W9-ABM-776

The Way I Say It

The Way I Say It

Nancy Tandon

Charlesbridge

Published by Charlesbridge
9 Galen Street
Watertown, MA 02472
(617) 926-0329
www.charlesbridge.com

Library of Congress Cataloging-in-Publication Data
Names: Tandon, Nancy, author.
Title: The way I say it / Nancy Tandon. Description: Watertown, MA:
    Charlesbridge, 2022. | Audience: Ages 10+. | Audience: Grades 4–6. |
    Summary: "Rory Mitchell has always had an issue saying his R's correctly
    (which is a real problem given his name); now in sixth grade his former
    best friend, Brent, suddenly sides with bullies against Rory; but then Brent
    is hit by a car and suffers a serious brain injury, which requires Rory to
    reevaluate everything."—Provided by publisher.
Identifiers: LCCN 2020051003 (print) | LCCN 2020051004 (ebook) |
    ISBN 9781623541330 (hardcover) | ISBN 9781632899118 (ebook)
Subjects: LCSH: Articulation disorders—Juvenile fiction. | Brain damage
    —Juvenile fiction. | Best friends—Juvenile fiction. | Bullying
    —Juvenile fiction. | Middle schools—Juvenile fiction. | CYAC: Speech
    therapy—Fiction. | Brain damage—Fiction | Best friends—Fiction. |
    Friendship—Fiction. | Bullying—Fiction. | Middle schools—Fiction. |
    Schools—Fiction.
Classification: LCC PZ7.1.T3754 Say 2022 (print) | LCC PZ7.1.T3754 (ebook) |
    DDC 813.6 [Fic]—dc23
LC record available at https://lccn.loc.gov/2020051003
LC ebook record available at https://lccn.loc.gov/2020051004

Printed in USA
(hc) 10 9 8 7 6 5 4 3 2 1

Display hand lettered by Jon Simeon and set in Love Ya Like a Sister Solid by
    Kimberly Geswein
Text type set in Minion Pro by Robert Slimbach
Color separations by Coral Graphic Services, Inc. in Hicksville, New York, USA
Printed by Berryville Graphics in Berryville, Virginia, USA
Production supervision by Jennifer Most Delaney
Designed by Jon Simeon

For Kate and Vijay, the two best characters I'll ever create

Hello, My Name Is . . .

I can't say my name. Not because it's a secret or anything. Honestly I'd shout it into a microphone right now if I could. I'd give up anything to be able to do that. Even my guitar-playing fingertip calluses, which took like a million hours to get. The first half-million hours hurt. A lot.

"Go ahead. Introduce yourself and tell us one fun thing you did this summer," Mrs. Nash repeats, as if I'm not answering because I forgot the instructions.

Standing in front of the class, I grip and release the fabric of my mesh shorts. I try to take a deep breath but manage only a fluttery gulp. I look toward the back of the room and focus on the crammed bookshelf and the ripped beanbag chair in front of it. Anything but all the faces staring at me. Waiting.

I glance at the clock. When the second hand reaches the ten, I'll do it.

No. I've already been up here too long. *Get it over with. Now!* Big breath. Tense tongue muscles. Squeeze the side edges hard against my teeth.

"I'm Wohwy." I push the words out on a rush of air.

Mrs. Nash bunches up her eyebrows and flicks her fingers through her short, spiky hair, taking forever to scan the class list before she looks back up. She says, "Oh, *Rory*. Here you are. Rory Mitchell."

Someone whispers. The already warm room suddenly seems ten degrees hotter.

"Well, *Rory*," she says, emphasizing the two *r*'s as if that will help me say them better, "what did you do for fun this summer?"

My mind starts to buzz like an amplifier set at max sound. I was hoping to skip this part. As nervous as I've been about starting a new school, I figured that by sixth grade the teachers would have knocked this question off their playlists.

I pretend to clear my throat, and the cough comes out as a dry little squeak. The clock ticks. Say something. Say something.

Just go with your gut. That's what my guitar teacher at music and arts camp always said when we were improvising. But I can't. I have to carefully choose what I say next. I force my brain to work, scanning for *r*'s and skipping any idea that has one: riding my bike, running my first 5K, going to Rhode Island. *Come on! Something without an* r*!*

Kids shift in their seats and the whispers spread.

"Let's give Rory our full attention, please," says Mrs. Nash.

Not helpful.

"I went to the beach," I manage to blurt out.

Mrs. Nash looks as relieved as I am when I'm done, and Melanie Franklin, whose desk is next to mine, stands up to take her turn. We've been in the same class since third grade, and her hairstyle has never changed. Two long, straight braids every day.

She won our school spelling bee in fourth *and* fifth grade. The girl is a human spell-check.

"I detest this," she whispers as we pass in the aisle. Up at the front, she tugs on her braids, and her words rush together. The only time she doesn't look completely tortured is when she tells us that today is her birthday.

I nod at her when she sits down, and she rolls her eyes and sticks her tongue out to the side. I settle into my chair and push my damp, sweaty hair up off my forehead. From the safety of my seat, I survey the room again. There are a ton of people I don't recognize, now that we're all mixed together for middle school. I see only four other kids from my elementary school—five if you count me, but I'm trying *not* to be seen.

Just then the door creaks open, and Brent Milliken walks in. "Sorry," he mumbles. "Locker."

I tense when he comes down my row, but he walks right by me like I'm invisible. He heads over to a chair next to a kid who didn't go to our old school. He looks kind of familiar, though.

"Saved you a spot, bro," the guy says, picking up a folder he'd put on the seat. His wide head is plopped right on top of massive shoulders stuffed into a green hoodie, and his hair is buzzed on the sides with a fuzzy yellow strip in the middle. He reminds me of a Minecraft cornstalk.

They bump fists. I try to hide my surprise by focusing on the "Welcome to Language Arts" handout in front of me. In the margin, I draw a bass-clef staff and start filling in a low, steady beat: *thwamm, thwamm, thwamm.*

"Everything okay back there, Rory?" asks Mrs. Nash. I look down at my clenched left fist and realize I'm pounding the desk.

I nod and turn my paper over. When the introductions start up again, I draw another music staff, treble clef this time. Then I fill in six simple notes.

I glance up occasionally. Kids parade to the front of the room in new sneakers and stiff first-day clothes. The room smells like clean laundry. Most girls are wearing boots and sweaters even though the real fall weather won't start for a while. It's like watching a back-to-school episode of the Fashion Network show *Who! What! When! WEAR! Why!* that Mom pretends not to be obsessed with.

We're coming to you live from Kensington Middle School in Lakeville, Connecticut! Or should I say Perfectville, Bob? Hahaha. Look at these wonderful students in the exact right clothes! And listen to their impeccable speech. Not one of them has any problem saying their own name. Well, almost *none of them.* (Cut to close-up of my mouth.) *Back to you in the studio, Bob.*

At least my turn is over, and I have lunch with Jett and Tyson to look forward to. After today, maybe I won't be so freaked out about meeting new people. At least that's what I tell myself.

The problem is, I don't really believe it. I'm supposed to go with my gut, right? Well, mine is seriously considering asking to be homeschooled.

When the bell rings, I tear off part of my paper and hand it to Melanie.

"What's this?"

Pointing to each quarter note, I hum: *hap-py birth-day to you.*

"Thank you!" she says, covering her smile with her hand. "You have extremely advanced doodling skills."

"That's me." I bow and wave for her to go first out the door.

I smile all the way to my next class, happy there's something I can do right.

Alphabetical Order

Things I used to be able to count on: Brent wanting to do the same stuff as me, Brent doing the talking whenever we were in new situations, and Brent being next to me in alphabetical order. We called ourselves the Michigan Twins, because of the *MI*'s—Mitchell and Milliken. Mom used to say we sounded like a law firm. But that was then.

Now as I worm my way through the wall of kids in the hallway, I wish my last name started with anything besides *M*. Brent is standing at the locker next to mine, twisting the dial of his combination and chewing on his lip. Shoulders hunched, he yanks down on the latch and slaps his palm against the locker when it doesn't budge, which makes me flinch.

"Stupid thing must be broken," he mumbles.

I've already got mine open. Brent looks from me to his lock and back again.

The warning bell rings. Brent gives his locker three swift kicks, as if breaking it might be the only way in.

"You have to pass the numbuh when you go left," I say just as Cornstalk comes up behind us and claps his hand down on Brent's shoulder with a loud smack.

"Yo, Milliken! You coming to wrestling tryouts today?" he asks.

"You know it."

"Hope you can take down your locker by then. Or maybe you need your little *fwend* to help?" He laughs in a loud blurt-snort combo.

When I glance over, my eyes are at the level of his sweaty pink forehead.

"Nah," says Brent. His locker finally clicks open, and he grabs a folder. "C'mon, let's go."

The tiny bit of okay I was feeling vaporizes.

"That's the kid from the bike path, right?" Cornstalk asks, glancing back at me as the two of them walk away.

"Yeah, total loser," I hear Brent say.

So that's where I've seen him before. The fact that Cornstalk was there that day feels like a knife in my belly, but it's Brent's words that make the blade twist. I force my language arts binder into my locker and slam the door.

"What's up with you?" asks Tyson, passing me on his way to second period.

"Idiots," I say, nodding toward where Brent and Cornstalk have stopped to talk to another guy.

"Dude, Brent Milliken is so last year. Forget about him."

Tyson knows that Brent and I stopped hanging out, but he doesn't know why. He's good about not being pushy like that. He starts humming and tapping to the beat of a song he made up this summer, and I can't help smiling.

"There you go," he says. "You know what I'm sayin'! Never let 'em see you drop. Don't sink to the bottom, gotta float to the top! Float on!" He thumps his chest with his fist, then points at me as he turns into his classroom.

I picture myself relaxing and floating down a river as I walk to my next class. In the glass hallway overlooking the courtyard, a kid I don't even know nods hello. Maybe this will work. *Go with the flow, Rory*, I tell myself. *Float.*

Me, Myself, and R

T he rest of the morning isn't so bad, especially because the next two teachers, Mr. Leigh in PE and Mrs. Lucas in math, take attendance by calling names off the list. I answer "yup" instead of "here"—learned that one a long time ago. My classes are easy to find because the main hallways make a big square around the courtyard. But there are so many new kids everywhere that by the time the bell rings for lunch, I feel like I've used up all the lives in my personal game of Please Don't Ask Me My Name. I'm relieved to meet up with Tyson and Jett inside the cafeteria.

"Isn't this place cool?" Tyson runs a finger along the zigzag design shaved on the back of his head as we check out the bright room full of clean, round tables.

"Epic upgrade. Oh, hang on—are those vending machines?" He takes off toward them.

"Let's join that platoon," says Jett, pushing up his glasses and pointing to a half-filled table behind a big pillar. "I know some of those guys from baseball."

Jett's part military the way I'm part Irish. It's just in him. He has a huge collection of army stuff that started with his great-grandpa's

World War II dog tags and grew from there. Back when we were show-and-tell age, everyone agreed that Jett brought in the coolest things. Today he's wearing a US Coast Guard cap he got at his cousin's graduation from the academy last year, and when we pass an older kid wearing a coast guard T-shirt, they nod at each other like they're in the same club.

I open my lunch and pull out dessert first. Taped to the top of the little plastic container is a note from my mom: *Have a sweet first day!* Classic Mom. Recruiting an innocent cupcake as an accomplice in her continuing quest to embarrass me.

"Oooh, what's that?" I hear a voice behind me.

For such a solid guy, Cornstalk has a pretty good stealth mode. I had no idea he was standing there. He reaches over and snatches the note, bumping our table hard enough to spill the chocolate milk Jett just opened.

"Oh, man, your mom still writes you *love notes*?" he says.

"Give that back!" My voice wobbles.

He turns to the laughing clump of kids behind him. I recognize a few of them. Wrestling friends of Brent's. "You know who this is, right?" he asks them.

One guy snorts and nods and another makes a hissing sound. Nerves jiggle through every part of me, except for my heart, which has stopped. This is not happening.

Cornstalk leans in and whispers to me, "I'll bet your mom still tucks love notes in your *diaper bag* too."

I go totally red.

"Mind your business, *Sherry*," says Tyson, pushing his way past the posse. He grabs the note out of Cornstalk's hand and shoves it into his pocket.

"Whatever. Rejects." Cornstalk walks away, and the other guys follow. They take over a big table in the back corner of the cafeteria, kicking out a few kids who made the mistake of sitting there.

"You *know* that kid?" I ask as Tyson scoots in next to me.

"Sort of." He tears into the fake-orange-colored peanut butter crackers he just bought. "His name's Danny Pulaski. Real genius, that guy. Speaks two languages: WWE and dirt bike. His mom used to be my dad's manager at the insurance company, so I'd have to hang out with him sometimes. Get this. His actual name is *Sheridan*, and his mom calls him *Sherry*. He hates that I know that."

Then Tyson leans in and motions us close. "And guess what else? His mom got fired and almost went to jail, like *real* jail, because she stole some money from the business."

"No way," says Jett. "Where'd you hear that?"

"From my dad! He had to talk in court and everything. And then Danny's dad flipped out on someone in the hallway of the courthouse, and *he* almost got arrested too. It was this whole big thing. Anyway, it ended up Danny's mom can't work at the insurance company anymore and has to pay all the money back. Of course, I'm not supposed to be telling you any of this." He zips his fingers across his lips.

"Whoa," I say.

I look over and see Danny slide out of his chair and chest-bump another guy, knocking the kid off balance. The two of them laugh and food spits out of Danny's mouth. At the same moment, the water I sipped goes down the wrong pipe, and I cough until my eyes water.

When the bell rings, we stop outside the cafeteria and pull out our schedules to see what's next.

"This is kind of confusing. Is it an A day? I think I have study hall," Jett says, reading from his.

"Same," says Tyson. "Specials are on B days. I'm pretty sure we go this way." He points toward where most kids are walking. "You with us, Rory?"

"Not today. Um . . . I've got speech."

"Ooh. That's tough," says Jett. He apologized when he stopped coming to speech at the end of last year for *ranking up and leaving his wingman.*

"Nah, I hear it's what all the cool kids do," I say.

Jett laughs and salutes me.

"That's right, man," says Tyson, tossing his water bottle from hand to hand. "Like I always say: float on."

After sneaking a look at my map, I walk alone down the long hallway that leads toward the gym. In elementary school, it seemed like there were basically two kinds of speech-therapy kids: the ones who got extra help on language arts stuff, and the ones who needed help making sounds.

I was the second kind, and at first I was in a big group of kids who all had messed-up speech, though mine was always the worst. We played games like Candy Land, practicing our sounds off flash cards before taking a turn. We stuck our tongues out for *th*, spit flying everywhere. Or we made cages with our teeth to *trap our slippery ssss snakes.* The speech room was basically a fun place to be.

Over the years kids started speaking correctly and leaving our group. By fourth grade it was just Jett and me. We were down to *r*'s and *l*'s, and Miss Lyn started talking to us about things like *respiration* and *articulation.*

She went over and over exactly where our tongues should be. Between your teeth for the *l*. Bunched up in back or tilted at the tip to make an *r*. We both eventually mastered *Louie licks lemon lollipops*. But only Jett got a handle on *Rosie's red rocking chair*. He could have started using his real name then, Jarrett, but by that time he'd decided he liked Jett better anyway. That was a *real relief*.

In fifth grade it was a lonely walk to speech therapy. Just me and my flunktacular *r*, in a solo session squished between Tamika Jones's raspy voice and a group called Lyn's Language Learners. I wanted so bad to say the dang sound and be done with trying to hide the reason I had to leave class every Monday and Wednesday at eleven thirty. I would contort my tongue and try to make it look exactly like the pictures in Miss Lyn's *Big Book of R*, but no matter what I did or how hard I worked, *r* always came out as *w*.

On the last day of fifth grade, Miss Lyn gave me a big hug and told me I'd love Mr. Simms, the speech guy at the middle school. "Really, everyone says he's super cool! And he's a whiz at his job. Auditory processing is his specialty, but he'll probably have you saying your *r* sound in no time!"

"Wonduhfulll," I'd said glumly, stretching out the *l* sound, which she sometimes made me review for "fun."

She winked at me and gave me a thumbs-up. I actually felt kind of sad saying goodbye to her.

As I get to the end of the hallway, the sound of squeaking sneakers from the gym mixes with the noisy band instruments warming up in a room nearby. I wish I could follow the music and hang out there all day. But guitar is not a school band instrument.

Anyway, I'm here. I look down and confirm the number on my schedule. Room A109. Next to the door is a small blue sign that says *Speech/Language Pathology*, and that's it. No apple-shaped "Welcome Back" poster, no construction-paper mouths with the names of students like Miss Lyn always had on her door.

I wipe my hands on my shorts and knock.

The Champ

No one answers. Through the door's small rectangular window, I can see a guy with his eyes closed, drumming on a desk with two pencils. He has headphones on. I look up and down the deserted hallway. I knock again, louder.

He opens the door and smiles. "Can I help you?"

I hold up my schedule. "Um. I'm supposed to come see you?"

"Oh, yes, yes . . . sure, of course. Rory, right? Come on in! I'm Mr. Simms."

He's wearing jeans and flip-flops. His white button-down shirt is hanging open, and he has a black T-shirt underneath that says *Metallica* on it. A little different from Miss Lyn's ready-for-church look.

The room is tiny. A massive pile of papers sits on a desk that's crammed into the corner next to a small sink. A laptop balances precariously on the pile. Mr. Simms motions for me to sit down at a wobbly table. He picks up his computer with one hand and starts sifting through the papers with the other. The only thing on the pale-yellow cinder-block walls is a poster of Yoda that says *Do or do not. There is no try.* There are two large spigots on the back wall with a mop bucket underneath. Next to the bucket is a shriveled plant that looks like it was left here all summer. I don't see Candy Land anywhere.

"Rory Mitchell. Here you are," he says, holding up a file.

He takes a moment to look at it. I wonder what's in there. Maybe a note that says *Tag, you're it! Great kid, hopeless* r. *Hugs, Miss L.*

"Says here you're a really hard worker." He smiles and pushes back his long curly hair. "I wish it said that in my file—haha!"

I'm not sure what to say to that.

"Listen." He closes the file and sits down backward in the chair next to mine. "You have trouble saying the *r* sound. It's driving you crazy. You've tried everything that anyone has ever suggested to you, and nothing's worked. You're sick of working with speech therapists, and you're pretty sure that I'll be as useless as all the others."

So he's a mind reader. "Well . . ." I start to answer.

"It's okay. I'm not offended. I'm not sure I can help you either, frankly. That *r* sound is my professional nemesis. Hate it. Very stubborn."

"So, why . . . ?" I start.

"Why are you here?" he finishes. "Good question. Why are you?"

"Um, because I have to be?" I'm not sure what this guy wants.

"Nope. Your grades are great. The fact that your speech isn't a hundred percent clear isn't affecting your schoolwork, so there's no law that says you need to come see me." He leans back, his hands clasped behind his head. "So, why are you here?"

"Because my mom makes a big deal about it?"

Mr. Simms laughs. "That might be part of it," he admits.

Then he stares at me for a moment, as if he's going to be taking a quiz later on what I look like.

"Do *you* want me to try to help you?" he finally asks.

I think about introducing myself in language arts this morning. And what happened at the lockers and at lunch.

"I just want to be able to say my name." The truth catches in my throat. "I wish I could change it completely."

"Why don't you?" asks Mr. Simms. His face is calm. He's serious.

"Can't," I say.

"Parents against it?" he asks.

"Well, basically. It's my uncle's name. Was. He, uh, died when I was little. My whole family has always said how happy it makes them that a bit of him is still alive, like, in me, you know? So I kinda can't ask to change it."

"Yeah, yeah, you've got a point there. That would definitely make you a . . . Well, that would not be good. It's also a pretty cool name, right?"

I shrug. Maybe. If I could say it.

He pulls on his chin. "So, you've got this great family name, but you have trouble with *r*'s. Tricky. Must be hard to meet new people."

Five minutes in, and this guy totally gets me. I relax a little.

"That's what I hate the most," I admit. "I tell them my name and then it's all, 'What? What did you say?' They don't do it to be mean, but sometimes I just want to yell, 'What's my *name*? You tell *me*. I just said it!'"

Mr. Simms jumps up from his chair and slams his hands on the table. "Oh. My. Gosh. I've *got* to show you something!" He takes the one step over to his desk. "You're not going to believe this. It's the greatest clip. *The greatest*—ha! Get it?" he asks.

I shake my head. I have no idea what he's talking about.

"What's my name? What's my name? Say my name!" he says, bending his knees into a lunge and throwing punches in the air. "You've got to see this!"

He grabs his laptop and sits down next to me. I watch him click around, then enter *Muhammad Ali* in the search bar.

"Wait till you see this," he mutters while the website is loading. "It's classic. Here it is!"

He taps the pause button on the screen. "Do you like M&M's?" he asks.

"Um, yup?" I say. Is this a test?

"Good." He pulls a giant bag out of his desk. "Me too. I've got a real sweet tooth."

He reaches in and grabs a huge handful. He pushes the bag across to me but then yanks it back abruptly.

"Allergies?" he asks. "Dairy? Lactose? Red dye 40?"

"Nope."

"Okay, then. Dig in! And watch this!"

We sit back with our M&M's, and an old black-and-white video clip of a boxing match begins.

"Muhammad Ali versus Ernie Terrell," Mr. Simms says, tapping their images on the screen. "Houston Astrodome, 1967. This was an epic fight between two world-class boxers. The greatest of all time, Muhammad Ali, is defending his heavyweight title. Terrell is the challenger."

Ali's dancing all over the ring. *Bam, bam, swish, dodge.*

"Now look! Right there! See what Ali's saying?" Mr. Simms pauses the video and rewinds a bit.

I lean in. I can see him yelling something, but I can't tell what.

When I shrug, Mr. Simms blurts out, "He's saying 'What's my name? What's my name?' See, he grew up as Cassius Clay. But when he converted his religion to Islam, he changed his name to Muhammad Ali. When Terrell refused to call him by his new name, Ali was so mad! Look, there it is again: 'What's my name?' Kapow!"

I see it, and I love it. We watch the rest of the clip in silence.

"So that's amazing, right?" says Mr. Simms, minimizing the computer screen. "You're just like him!" He's grinning and nodding at me.

What? "Uh, not so much," I say. "One, he doesn't seem to need any help talking. And two, wasn't he, like, famous?"

"Sure, sure," says Mr. Simms. "But he got mad when people bugged him about his name, just like you."

He pauses and winks. "And look what happened to them."

Aren't teachers supposed to say things like "hands are not for hitting"? I picture myself sparring with Danny, then standing over him after a knockout punch.

The bell rings for fifth period.

"Okay, see you later then, Rory," says Mr. Simms, closing his laptop and jamming the candy bag back into his drawer.

"Um, okay," I say. "Anything I should do until next time?" Miss Lyn always sent me away with a homework log and lists of words to practice.

"Yeah," he says. "Work on your right hook." He takes a fake swing at my head.

I duck, not sure yet if this guy is for real. But I do know that for the first time since the good old Gumdrop Forest days, I wish speech therapy lasted longer.

Contagious

I'm starting to feel better about making it through the day. Only two more classes and I'm outta here.

Brent and Danny and some other guys turn the corner right as I close the speech-therapy door behind me. I try to blend into the wall until they pass, but apparently I forgot to take my camouflage pills this morning. Danny looks at the blue plaque next to the door, and his eyes light up.

"Have fun learning to talk, *Wohwy*?" he asks.

Some of the others laugh.

"Give me a bwake," I say. Immediately I want to suck the word back in. *Nice job! Give him more ammunition! Good thinking.* My skin starts to tingle.

Brent stares at the floor and kicks the plastic strip at the bottom of the wall, his sneaker leaving a little black mark every time it hits.

"Come on," he says. "We're gonna be late."

"Hey, you heard him: he needs a *potty bwake*," says Danny. "Maybe you need one too?"

"As if," says Brent, backing away. He's got this look that says, *I don't want to catch what you have, plague boy.*

I press my hands against my legs to keep them from shaking. The two-minute warning bell rings.

"Whatever. Let's go." Danny turns and clips my shoulder, sending me thudding into the wall. More laughter.

"Everything okay out here?" asks Mr. Simms, popping his head into the hallway.

The laughing stops, and Danny squints at me.

"Fine," I say, willing Mr. Simms not to make it worse.

"Well, that's good." Mr. Simms moves around our little clump, staring at each of us. "Because at yesterday's staff meeting, your principal, Mr. Perkins, specifically asked all the teachers to cover our PRIDE expectations in homeroom this morning. Preparation. Respect. Individuality. Development. Excellence. Remember that?"

We all nod and mumble, except Danny, who stays silent.

"Sixth graders are expected to *consistently demonstrate* respectful behavior," Mr. Simms says directly to him.

Danny responds with a sharp nod.

"Okay, off you go."

The group shuffles away, and Mr. Simms grabs my sleeve and whispers, "See you in the next round, champ."

When I get home that afternoon, I stand next to the school-bus-shaped cake that Mom insisted on making "once more for old time's sake" and force a smile for a photo. She's been baking a cake like this since I was in kindergarten and was freaked out about riding the bus. I could have asked her not to make it this year, but hey, it's *cake*—and Mom thinks starting a new school year is always something to celebrate. Her eyes are bright, and she's fluttering her fingers on the countertop.

"So, how was it?" she asks as I take a huge bite. As embarrassing as Mom's thematic baking is, it's also delicious.

"Did you have fun? Did you meet some new friends?" Mom's always pushing me to *Speak up! Introduce yourself! Put yourself out there!* Easy for her to say. Her name's Patty.

"Mom, it was fine. It was school. How fun could it be?"

"Hey, count your blessings," says Mom. "There are a lot of kids in other countries who would love to be in your shoes."

More classic Mom. And she knows what she's talking about too, because she writes the newsletter for a group called GEE, which stands for Global Education Equality. That's one of Mom's many passions.

"Okay, okay. It was a life-changing day, and I'm feeling blessed," I say in a robot voice. "Can I go now?"

She smirks and playfully smacks the side of my head. "I see you're smarter already. Fine, you *may* go. I have to get back to my computer anyway."

I'm almost to the steps when she says, "Wait, before I forget: Mr. Garland was telling me today that he misses hearing you practice piano."

"Mom . . ."

"No, no, I'm not saying take up piano again. A deal's a deal. I'm just saying, he enjoyed hearing you play. So, think about it? Sometime when you see him out on the porch?" she says.

Mr. Garland has been our neighbor forever. The houses on our street were built close together, with almost identical front lawns. It's our backyards that are special because they all connect to a patch of town land that can never be developed. Right now, the trees are so thick with green that we can't see the houses on the street behind us at all, so we have some privacy. But that will change once the leaves start changing color and falling.

Mr. Garland is retired and lives alone, and he's almost always out on his screened-in side porch, which is right next to our living-room window. Even in the middle of winter, he'll be out there in his big puffy coat "taking some air."

Sometimes when I was playing piano and the window was open, I'd hear Mr. Garland singing along to songs like "You're a Grand Old Flag" and "God Bless America." (My piano teacher was very patriotic.) If I heard Mr. Garland, I'd make sure I practiced those songs an extra-long time, even if I didn't need to.

"Okay, Mom. Maybe a few songs. If I see him."

"Good enough," she says, and hands me a plate with a second piece of cake. "Here. Take another. I have no idea when or what dinner's going to be."

Up in my room, I drop my backpack on the floor. I'm supposed to fill out a long "get to know you" form for language arts, but I can't focus on work with all the bad parts of today swirling inside me. Instead, I pick up my guitar and sink into my beat-up recliner. With the amplifier set on one, the tinny twangs of all the notes I pluck are just for me. I ease into the opening solo of AC/DC's "Thunderstruck." It's tricky, and I'm still pretty slow at it, but I go over and over the notes, my fingers moving around the neck of the guitar, dancing around the frets. For a moment the music completely covers me, blocking out everything else.

When I'm done, I let the last note hang in the air until only the low buzz of the amp is left. I reach over and turn it off. I wish it were that easy to switch off my feelings too.

Passing Notes

A sweet candy smell makes me turn from my locker with a smile.

"Hi, Rory," says Jenna. The cartoon chicken on her T-shirt is holding a sign that says *I am not a nugget.*

There are a lot of good things about Jenna Kim. Number one: she smells like butterscotch.

"Hi, Jenna. How's it going?"

"Good. I'm on my way to science. I have Mr. Griggs first period. He told us we're going to start doing a molecular mud unit today!" she replies.

Number two: she's not afraid of a little dirt.

"Yeah, that's gonna be gweat," I say.

"I know, right?"

Number three: she's never, not once, asked me to repeat myself.

She scans the row of lockers. Her shiny black hair, with a new thin blue streak in it, swishes back and forth across her shoulders.

"So, um, does Brent Milliken have a locker around here?" she asks.

"Yeah, he's next to me," I say, pointing. "Why?"

"Oh, uh, okay. Well, someone wanted me to give him this note. I can't tell you who." She holds up an impossibly tiny folded piece of paper.

"Oh." I watch pink spots grow on each of her cheeks as she looks past me down the hallway.

"Here he comes. This is so awkward. I can't. Here, Rory. You do it." She shoves the note into my hand and bolts toward the science room, dodging oncoming kids.

"Thanks! See you in math!" she calls from the doorway.

The last time I delivered a note to Brent, it was through the mail the summer after fourth grade. We were supposed to go to camp together, but Brent broke his leg. At the camp store, I bought a pack of stamped postcards that had photos of fruit with funny faces painted on them and sent one to him every day with a joke written on it. Like, one was this orange with puckered-up lips, and I wrote, "Orange you glad you're not as ugly as this guy?" He said he wrote back, and I figured I must have already left camp by the time his letter got there. But now I wonder.

When he gets to his locker, Brent ignores me. I'm *a total loser*. He turns his back and shuffles his folders around. The little triangle of paper in my hand turns into a grenade. I pull the pin.

"Uh, Bwent?"

He looks over his shoulder instead of answering me.

I keep going anyway. "Jenna gave me this note. To give to you."

"Oh." He snatches it and stuffs it into his pocket.

"Yowah welcome," I say after he turns and leaves.

"Talking to your imaginary friend?" asks Danny, walking past me.

The warning bell rings for first period.

"Let's go, people," says Mr. Griggs, leaning into the hallway from the science lab.

I have no choice but to skulk along behind Danny on our way to language arts. I stare at his fancy basketball shoes and wish I could trip him with my mind.

At lunch I'm glad to take my usual spot between Jett and Tyson. Tyson's spinning a quarter on its edge. He's never not moving.

"What's up?" I ask.

"All present and accounted for," says Jett, squirting ketchup from a little packet onto his gray hamburger. "One hundred and seventy-eight more mornings to go. Morale is low."

I open my lunch and hand them each a wrapped piece of leftover cake.

"Dude. Nice!" says Tyson, immediately peeling it open to lick the frosting.

"Best tradition ever," says Jett.

"Hi, guys," says Jenna, stopping at our table.

Melanie is behind her, scanning the lunchroom.

Jenna looks down at Jett's burger. "Ugh, Jett! How can you eat that? Not only is it meat, but it's the nastiest meat." Jenna has forever been trying to get people to join her on Team Vegetarian.

"Like this," says Jett, taking a big bite.

She sticks her tongue out at him.

"Hi, Melanie!" says Tyson.

"Greetings, C-O-M-P-A-T-R-I-O-T." Melanie nods at him to take a guess. This is their game.

"Compatriot—someone who loves their country?"

"Sort of," says Melanie. "We're sixth-grade *compatriots* now; we both inhabit this new school."

Tyson nods at her with a serious face, as if it's the word he's interested in.

Then Melanie nudges Jenna, who leans over and asks, "Rory— did you, um, deliver the package?"

She half whispers the last part into my ear, and it tickles my neck. I cover the spot with my hand. "Yeah, he got it."

"Good, thanks." She straightens up and tucks her hair behind her ear. "See you guys later."

Melanie grabs a fry from Tyson's tray as they leave. "Bye!"

"Melanie Franklin just ate one of my fries," Tyson says. "One of *my* fries!"

"Congratulations," Jett says. "Let me know when the wedding is." He turns toward me. "What did Jenna want?"

"Nothing."

"I think she likes you."

"Not likely." But I watch her walk away and maybe wish she did.

She and Melanie go across the room and circle around the table where Brent is sitting. He glances up at them but then looks away without making room.

I rewind to last year, to the first time I realized Brent hadn't saved me a seat at lunch the way he usually did. Two guys from another class flanked him, and they were all wearing identical Bantam Wrestling warm-up jackets. He had just joined the town team.

I shot him a look to ask what was going on, but he was staring at his sandwich like it was the most interesting food in the universe. He nodded along to whatever the other guys were saying. When I moved toward an open spot nearby, someone slid into it before I could. The teacher on lunch duty was nagging me to find a place to sit, and since none of my other friends had lunch that period, I ended up eating alone.

When I asked him about it later, Brent told me I was making a big deal out of nothing. He said he hadn't even seen me and didn't know what I was talking about. I believed him at first because I wanted to. But that was before he did the thing that made believing anything he said impossible. I still hate thinking about it.

I wish I could shake my head like an Etch A Sketch and start completely clear. But it's only day two of sixth grade, and my screen's already messed up. A shout of laughter coming from Brent and Danny's table makes the two little dials spin faster.

Float Like a Butterfly

The hallway hums and reverberates with sounds coming from the speech room. The drumbeat thumps inside me, covered by an epic layer of tight, pulsating guitar and Mr. Simms's loud voice, singing a song I know about *light* and *night*. I peek through the window and call his name to let him know I'm there, but he's so into playing air guitar that he doesn't hear me.

I wait until the song ends and then give three sharp knocks.

Mr. Simms pulls the door open and peers up and down the hallway. "Anyone else hear that?"

"I don't think so," I say.

"Sweet. Here, come on in, come on in."

Mr. Simms is red and sweaty. "Don't mind me," he says. "Sometimes I pep myself up with a little dance party." He points to the cover art on his laptop. "Metallica. You know them?"

"A little bit. Well, I know that song anyway. I learned part of it at music camp."

"That's excellent! What do you play?" He sits down and pats the chair next to him.

I make a strumming motion, avoiding the word *guitar*.

"Nice! What's your favorite kind of music?" he asks.

"Hmm. I listen to all kinds of stuff. Lately a lot of AC/DC. My dad loves them."

"Ah, hard rock. Solid."

"I like heavy metal too. Avenged Sevenfold, Slipknot. Actually anything that makes me feel good." I like this conversation.

"Awesome! That's the way to be a music fan, Rory. I knew I liked you. Here, take this." He writes *Metallica, 1991, aka the black album* on a piece of paper and hands it to me.

"Look up their fifth album when you get home. Amazingly genius stuff. Have a listen and let me know what you think."

"Okay, cool." I pull my music-staff notebook out of my backpack and open it to slide the note inside.

"Whoa!" says Mr. Simms, placing his hand on the page so I can't close it. "What's that?"

"Oh. Just a few lines, ideas I have for songs."

"No kidding? Man, I wish I could read music. I have an old drum set I kick around on once in a while. But you know what? I've always wanted to learn guitar. How long have you been at it? You any good?" he asks.

"I'm okay. I've been playing since I was nine on my dad's old acoustic. The deal was if I put in my time with piano, I could get my own electwic. So that's what I play on now."

"I'm impressed, Rory." Mr. Simms hums and drums his fingers on the table, twisting his swivel chair side to side.

I wait for him to get out *The Big Book of R*, or some game, or a worksheet.

"Rory who can't say *r*," he says. "Mr. Guitar Rock Star."

"Yup." I like the way that sounds, even with all the *r*'s.

"What are we going to do with you?"

"Is it too late to switch to Islam? I could get a new name like Cassius Clay did," I offer up.

"Hmmm." Mr. Simms goes over to his shelf and runs his finger along the book spines. There must be at least a dozen about Muhammad Ali. "I'm a bit of a fan," he admits, taking one down.

He stands there, reading quietly and flipping pages. I glance at the clock. What kind of speech session is this? Finally he says, "Here we go!"

He puts the book on his desk and holds up his fists. Reading from the open page, he says, "'Clay swings with his left, Clay swings with his right, look at young Cassius carry the fight.'"

"What?" I have no idea what's going on.

"Some people say Muhammad Ali was the original rapper. There are a ton of rhymes attributed to him. They called him the 'Louisville Lip.'" He takes out an index card and copies the lines from the book.

"Here." He hands it to me.

I read the card out loud. "'Clay swings with his left, Clay swings with his wight, look at young Cassius cawwy the fight.'"

"Good try. Now, that *r* in *carry* is a toughie because it's right in the middle. So, let's work on *right*. Stand up."

I hesitate. No worksheets? No board game?

"Come on, come on, on your toes, Lakeville Lip." He's got his hands on his hips like a superhero.

I stand up, and he pushes the small table as much out of the way as possible in the tiny room.

"Just shift your weight," he says. "Side to side. Sway. You've gotta dance like Ali."

I start wobbling like an off-balance robot.

"Now read the card again," he says.

I hold the card up and stand still.

"No, no, no, you've got to keep moving."

I sway more slowly so I can read at the same time. "'Clay swings with his left, Clay swings with his wight, look at young Cassius cawwy the fight.'"

"Nice. But you're still way too tense. Loosen up! Dance a little! Ali used to say, 'Float like a butterfly, sting like a bee; you can't hit what you can't see.' I need you to *float*!"

There's Tyson's word again. I try to relax and dip my knees a little more this time, rocking back and forth. "Clay swings with his left, Clay swings with his wight, look at young Cassius cawwy the fight."

"That's what I'm talking about," says Mr. Simms. "Good work."

"But I'm still saying *w*," I say, looking down.

"Well, for now. But you're having fun, right?" He drags the two chairs so they're facing each other. "C'mon back and sit down."

From his desk drawer, he pulls out a small flashlight. "I hope you didn't have onions for lunch."

"Nope."

"Good. I need to look inside your mouth and see exactly what's going on in there, okay? Try a few sounds for me, Rory. *Grrr.* Let me get a look at your growl."

I do the best I can while he leans in and stares.

"Now, *arrrgh.* Give me your best pirate." He's right up in my face.

He asks me to say the sounds again and again while he shines his flashlight around and tilts his head to look from different angles. Finally he sits back.

"Okay, we'll start with what we can get. There are a lot of different ways to make the *r* sound. And the position of your tongue often depends on what sounds are going on around it. But you've got a lot of potential, Rory, really. I don't think we'll have to change your name. We'll get you sorted before the big moment on Step-Up Day, I promise."

"What do you mean?" I ask. My float starts to sink.

"At the end of the year, sixth and seventh graders have a ceremony to move up a year. Then the eighth graders have their graduation that night. It's really fun," he explains.

"But why would *I* have to say anything?" I roll the card in my hand into a tight coil.

"Oh, it all started a few years back when the Glidden quadruplets came through. Same last name, of course. But they all had these complicated, similar first names. Micheala, Mykendra, Makensie, and, oh, I forget the fourth. Anyway, someone brought it up with the principal's office, and Mr. Perkins decided that all the students would just announce themselves onstage so there wouldn't be any screwups. Turned out people liked it that way, so it's kind of a tradition now. Then kids started adding a little flair, like wearing their sports jerseys or their school-play costumes, doing a few dance steps, that kind of thing. Everyone loves it." He looks way too excited about this thing that terrifies me.

The bell rings, but I don't move. I'm going to hide here all year until that ceremony is over. Mr. Simms puts his hand on my slumped shoulder.

"Hey, don't worry about Step-Up. It's an entire school year away! One thing at a time. But keep that card with you, okay? We'll work on it again next session."

I linger at the door, checking out the hallway status.

Mr. Simms comes up behind me. "Did you know Muhammad Ali got picked on as a kid?"

"No way."

"Yup. In fact, one of the reasons he got into boxing was because someone stole the bike he'd gotten for his birthday. He was so mad, and he wanted to get even. But this cop told him, 'You'd better learn to fight first.' And that's when he started going to a gym. Tell you what: I'd hate to be that thief if Ali the Champ ever found out who he was!"

"Yeah," I say, smiling.

"Just keep your feet moving," he says, nudging me out the door.

He starts whistling, and I turn back. "Bon Jovi?"

He nods. "'Livin' on a Prayer,' man."

The tune follows me all the way down the hall, and I can still hear him whistling even after I turn the corner.

Dad

"**G**ood news!" Mom says on Saturday morning as she slides a pancake onto my plate.

Dad and I are sitting next to each other on stools across the counter from her. It's chilly in the kitchen, so I lean over the steam rising off my warm breakfast.

"Oh?" asks Dad, looking up from scrolling through the sports highlights on his phone.

I push aside the real maple syrup and grab the fake kind. Mom makes a face but avoids going into the whole "processed sugar" lecture like she used to do when she was blogging twice a month for ANNA's Way (All Natural/No Additives). The only reason I can still drown my pancakes in high-fructose goodness is that Dad backed me up by reminding Mom that he didn't like the real kind when he was a kid either.

"I got a call from Stephanie Milliken," says Mom.

At the word *Milliken*, a pancake bite lodges in my throat. *Mayday, Mayday. Goin' down.* I reach for some emergency OJ.

"What did she want?" I ask.

"Well, we were talking about how long it's been since we've gotten the old preschool gang together. All the moms and kids are going to go over to the Millikens' after school on Tuesday to catch up."

"Remind me: Who's in this *gang*?" asks Dad.

"Rory, Brent, Sunil, and Thomas. Those four were inseparable on the playground! And we moms used to be quite close too. Then Thomas and Sunil went to the magnet school, and the boys all had different activities. I can't wait to see everyone."

"I'm gonna be busy on Tuesday," I say.

"With what?" asks Mom.

"Things."

"Ah, things. Well, we should definitely decline this kind invitation. So what if friendship is the honey on the bread of life?" Her sarcasm game is good sometimes.

"Mom. Stop."

"C'mon. It'll only be a few hours. Why don't you want to see those guys?" Mom fills a small pink pitcher from her pig collection with her own syrup and puts it into the microwave to warm.

I want to look my parents in the eye and tell them what happened last year. And what's going on at school now. But I don't know where to start. And it's hard to talk about that kind of thing with Dad. Whenever I try, he always changes the subject or starts talking in sports lingo. Dad and I are a great team when it comes to things like shooting hoops or bonding over syrup, but not so much with anything that has to do with feelings or speech problems—or any problems, really. I press my fingers against my eyelids until I see colors.

"Rory?" asks Dad. "You okay?"

I look up and notice a worried glance between the two of them.

"Yeah, I'm fine. I haven't been hanging out with Bwent as much lately, that's all." Right. Brent Milliken is probably freaking out right now too and begging his mom to call off Tuesday's plan.

"Well, I know you two didn't get together over the summer because of camps and vacations, but this will give you a chance to reconnect." Mom accidentally tips over her Miss Piggy saltshaker. She licks her finger to pick up the grains and flicks them over her left shoulder.

"And I haven't seen Thomas or Sunil since I was, like, five," I protest.

"That's why it'll be so good to see them again!"

"Mom! Will you please stop? Just quit with all this stuff!"

"What stuff?" she asks. She seems genuinely confused.

"Notes in my lunch! Deciding who I'll hang out with! I'm not a little kid!"

Mom puts a hand over her heart.

"You put a note in his lunch bag?" Dad says after a beat of silence.

"Excuse me for wanting to wish my son a good first day of school," says Mom.

"Honey, no. I was a sixth-grade boy once. Trust me. No notes," Dad says.

"Thank you," I say, holding my hands out, palms up.

"Rory's growing up. He needs space." Dad folds his arms, and Mom gives him a *we'll see about that* look.

Dad turns to me. "But we're also in charge. You're going Tuesday. End of story."

I spend the rest of the morning in the basement playing an online game with Tyson and Jett. We take turns setting each other up to decimate our virtual enemies with the push of a button. It's so easy to tell in Zombocalypse who's on your side and who's not.

"Rory! That's enough screen time!" Mom yells from the top of the stairs.

"Just let us finish this level!"

"Listen to your mother," says Dad, which is ironic because he pretty much spends every Saturday glued to a screen himself, watching whatever sport is in season.

"Gotta go," I say to the guys through my headset.

I shut off the console and trudge up the stairs to the living room, where Dad is sitting on the couch flipping through channels. He used to try to get me to watch games with him. I know he wishes he were coaching me on a bunch of different teams—he's been telling me that since he put up a basketball hoop over our garage when I turned six. But I think he's finally settled for playing one-on-one or HORSE with me in the driveway.

My dad's friends always shout "Mitch!" when they see him, like they're cheering from the stands. They love to thump him on the back and talk about all these great sports things he did in high school and college. Even now, if they invented a new sport, my dad would score a goal the first time he played. He's that guy. The thing is, I could probably be that guy too, if I worked at it. It's not like I get picked last in PE or anything. But the only thing I've ever been interested in long enough to get good at is music. Dad seemed disappointed about that at first, until I started to be able to play along when he'd put on AC/DC. I mean, who can deny the excellence that is the opening bars of "For Those About to Rock (We Salute You)"?

The deep-green carpeting squishes between my toes, and I flop down across the puffy chair, dangling my legs over the arm.

"Hey, wait, go back to that," I say, catching a glimpse of something as he clicks through the channels.

Dad flips back to a car race. "This?"

"Go back one more. Is that Muhammad Ali?"

"Yeah, 'the Greatest,'" says Dad with a surprised smile. "You interested?"

He slides over and pats the cushion next to him. A voice-over is telling us how important this fight, the Rumble in the Jungle, was to Ali's career.

"The other guy is George Foreman. He was the world heavyweight champion at the time," says Dad, then he chuckles. "He ended up making a ton of money selling those indoor grill things. But this was mid-1970s, way before all that."

On the screen we watch clips of the two boxers going at each other, leather gloves pounding into sweaty skin. *Fwap-fwap-fwap.*

"Looks like Ali's taking the most hits," I say.

Dad looks over at me with a grin. "Wait for it. Ali's just letting Foreman wear himself out. Now look—watch this—look at Foreman getting all tired and sloppy!"

The show cuts to the end of the fight. The static-filled audio of the announcer gets louder and faster as he gives the play-by-play. I lean forward on the couch, my body bobbing up and down like I'm in the ring with the boxers. Finally, out of nowhere, Ali lands a direct hit, and Foreman stumbles and falls to the ground.

"Did you *see* that?" Dad asks. "That is *the* moment Ali regained the heavyweight title."

I leap up from the couch. "'Clay swings with his left, Clay swings with his wight, look at young Cassius cawwy the fight.'" I bounce a little and punch the air.

Dad turns to me with big eyes. "Yes!" he says.

You'd think I'd been the one to knock out George Foreman.

"Where'd you hear that?" he asks.

"Um, well, Mistuh Simms has a thing for Muhammad Ali," I say.

"Mr. Simms?"

"My new speech guy." I look down.

"Huh," says Dad.

I wait for him to follow up with something about how I need to keep swinging for the fences.

"Well. He sounds like a smart guy."

"He'd bettuh be. He's my Obi-Wan. My only hope," I say.

Dad laughs and pulls me back down onto the couch with him.

After the show ends, I wander over toward the window next to the piano and pull back the striped curtain. In our side yard, the maple tree's leaves are starting to turn orangey red. Mr. Garland is on his porch reading. I crack open the window and pull out one of my old piano books. I bang away for a little while on the "Marines' Hymn." My fingers go up and down the keyboard from the halls of Montezuma to the shores of Tripoli. When I finish I can hear Mr. Garland's cane still thumping the beat.

Robots

"**H**ello!" Mrs. Milliken chirps when she opens her door. "It is *so* good to *see* you!"

She gives my mom a big hug, then turns and puts her hands on my shoulders and squints at me. "Rory! Wow! You really grew this summer, huh? You're so tall!"

I smile with my lips closed, biting the inside of my cheek. I wonder how much Brent has told her, if anything.

She steps back and motions for us to come in. "Welcome! Welcome! I can't wait to catch up!"

The Millikens live a few streets over from us, where all the backyards are tiny because the houses are so big. McMansions, Mom calls them.

"So good to see you too, Stephanie!" says Mom. "Your home looks beautiful!" Mom's voice echoes around their giant two-story entryway.

"Thank you! I *finally* got those custom blinds for that sliding door. Come see!"

We follow Mrs. Milliken into the kitchen.

I look each of the other moms right in the eye and say, "Hi, Mrs. Chawla. Hi, Mrs. Dowd. Nice to see you." I hope this will get me points with Mom, so maybe we can leave early.

"Rory! You're here!" Brent's little sister, Maggie, pops her head out from under the kitchen table and waves a sparkly pink wand at me. "Want to come to my tea party?"

"Oh, hi, um . . ."

"Maggie, Rory is here to play with the big kids. All the boys are in the basement, Rory. Go on down," says Mrs. Milliken.

Truthfully I'd rather hide under the table with Maggie.

I take the stairs one slow step at a time, like a person in a horror movie investigating a spooky noise. When I get to the bottom, the guys are staring straight ahead, playing a video game. This is good.

"Hi, Rory," says Sunil, glancing over. "Hurry, you're on my team."

He dips his body to one side as his guy on the big-screen TV does the same.

"Special-Ops Station Nine," says Thomas. "Level six."

"Got it," I say, picking up the fourth controller.

It's not hard for me to jump into the game, and as a team Sunil and I do all right. No one says much, except for things like "Watch out!" and "Get that ammo!" and "Dude, I so got you!" Brent doesn't say anything.

I would have been happy playing that game all afternoon, but after a while Mrs. Milliken calls down and says, "Boys! It's a gorgeous day! Why don't you all come up and spend some time outside? I've got ice cream for you."

We finish the level we're on and head upstairs. Mrs. Milliken gives us each an ice-cream sandwich as we go out to the backyard.

"Do you have any rope?" Thomas asks.

"Maybe in the garage. Why?" asks Brent.

"I'm taking this magic class from a guy who performs at parties and stuff. I could show you a really cool trick," Thomas answers.

"Right, 'cause magic tricks are cool," mumbles Brent.

Sunil lifts his eyebrows, but Thomas acts like he didn't hear.

We walk around to the front of the house. Brent opens the garage door, and the four of us start poking through the shelves and in the laundry baskets Mrs. Milliken has out there to organize all the junk. Sunil finds an old model rocket and starts to tinker with the launcher.

"Look what I found!" says Thomas. "I can't believe you still have this!"

He holds up the "robot" that Brent and I made together in preschool. I remember thinking we were building something amazing that would actually work. Now I can see that it is just a walkie-talkie duct-taped to a roller skate, decorated with pipe cleaners.

"Yeah, well, my mom saves everything," says Brent.

"Rory, remember when you guys brought this in for show-and-tell and told us you were going to ask it to clean your rooms for you?" asks Sunil.

I pause at how incredibly familiar all of this is. Of course I remember. We spent hours playing with that stupid thing.

"No," I say. "No, I don't."

I grab the toy and send it flying down the steep driveway toward the street. It flips over and the antenna breaks off when it hits the edge of the sidewalk.

"Okaaay," says Thomas. He gives one more glance around the garage. "Well, no rope here. You guys wanna play manhunt?"

"Sure," says Sunil.

"Fine," I say.

"Whatever," says Brent.

For the first few rounds, we find each other easily. When it's Sunil's turn to be the seeker, I wedge myself deep into the thick row of perfectly square bushes in the front yard and wait. Sunil finds Brent and then Thomas. All three of them are looking for me when I hear another, different voice call "Yo!"

I peek out and see Danny turning his bike into Brent's driveway.

"'Sup?" Brent asks, walking toward him. He looks over his shoulder at Sunil and Thomas.

Danny looks at them and says, "Dude. What are you *doing*?"

"My mom is having some of her old friends over, so these guys came too," says Brent.

"We all went to preschool together," says Thomas. "And Rory Mitchell. We're trying to find him."

"Yeah, *wight*," says Brent. "More like trying *not* to find him." He shoots a silencing glare at Thomas.

"*Wight?*" says Danny, laughing. "Anyway, bummer, dude. I was going to ask you to ride around with me, but it looks like you're busy with your preschool playtime."

"I don't even want to be here," says Brent. "Let me get my bike."

I think about busting out of the bush and announcing to everyone what Tyson told me about Danny's mom being a thief. But as Danny launches a wad of spit onto the ground, I sink back farther. *You can't hit what you can't see.*

I watch through a screen of tight green leaves as Brent comes back with his bike and the two of them ride off. Thomas and Sunil don't even try to keep looking for me. They both go inside.

I pull myself out from my hiding spot and head toward the house. On the way I kick the little garden gnome in the front yard, knocking it over.

We all leave pretty soon after that. Mrs. Milliken practically falls over herself apologizing to us for her son taking off.

"We'll have to do this again sometime!" she calls from the porch. "I'll let you ladies know when I'm headed to the outlets next! Shopping day!" She waves so hard that the skin on her arm flaps.

"Did you have fun?" Mom puts the car into reverse.

"No, Mom. No, I did not have fun." I scowl.

As she pulls out of the driveway, we crunch over the broken walkie-talkie.

"What was that?" she asks, craning to see.

"Nothing," I say. "Just some junk."

Upside Down

Mom angles the rearview mirror so she can see me. Her eyes flit back and forth between the road and my reflection. Her eyebrows are pulled in tight, pressing a deep wrinkle between them. "What happened?" she asks.

"Nothing. Let's just go home," I say.

"Are you mad because Brent left?"

"Him leaving was the only good thing. I nevuh want to see him again." I cross my arms and tuck my chin.

We pull up to a stop sign, and Mom turns around to look at me. "Did something happen, Rory? Did he make fun of your speech?"

The little muscle at the bottom of her eye twitches, the way it does whenever she gets worked up about something. I decide not to go into the details.

"Mom. No. Geez. He just doesn't want . . . He's not my fwend. Doesn't want to be. That's all," I say.

"Since when?" Her voice is high and pinched, and her knuckles are white against the steering wheel.

"I don't know. I don't want to talk about it."

Mom stops asking questions, but I can see her sneaking looks at me. I keep hearing Brent say he hoped they wouldn't find me. I hear him calling me a loser. And I hear what he said on that awful day last spring. I grip the door handle and bang my knee on the back of the seat. Mom flinches but stays quiet.

When we get home, I bolt from the car, stomp up the stairs, and slam my bedroom door. I need to *not* think. I plug in my earbuds and turn on the Metallica album Mr. Simms told me about, cranking up the volume so that the crashing noise fills my head.

Halfway through the fourth track, Mom cracks open the door and peeks in.

I pull the buds out of my ears. "What?" I snap. "I said I don't want to *talk* about it!"

"Excuse you?" Her eyes narrow and she holds up the phone, pressing it between her palms. Then she softens her voice to a whisper. "It's Tyson."

I give her an *I'm sorry* look. "Can you tell him I'm busy?"

She takes a breath and holds it for a moment.

"Please? Mom, I can't."

"Fine," she says with a frown.

She shuts the door, and I hear her murmuring into the phone. I reposition my earbuds and slouch down in my recliner, closing my eyes. I just want to be completely alone. I stay that way until the album ends. When I open my eyes, the sky outside my window has faded to gray.

There's a soft knock on my door.

"Mom, I don't want to talk to Tyson. I don't want to talk to anyone. Just say I'm sleeping."

She opens the door anyway. Her face looks weird, like she's about to be sick. I sit up. "Mom?"

She walks over, kneels down, and grabs me in a tight hug.

"Mom, stop squishing me! What the heck?"

She unwraps her arms and puts one hand on either side of my face. "Dad just called from the hospital."

No surprise there, because that's where Dad works, in the billing department. But Mom's eyes are watery, and she almost never cries.

"Brent Milliken was admitted. He was riding his bike and got hit by a car," she says.

"What?"

"It's serious." Her voice is shaky and wet. "Dad was walking out the main doors, and he saw Mr. Milliken come in. So of course he stayed and helped him find where they'd taken Brent."

She starts to cry. "He'd come in by LifeFlight copter. We don't know much else right now, but the fact that they had to call the helicopter . . ." She fades out and hugs me again.

I let her hang on for a long time. Seeing your mom cry is just about the worst thing in the world. I know I should be upset too. But instead I feel nothing. I don't know which is worse.

Cards and Candles

At school the next day, Brent's accident is all anyone can talk about. Kids are hanging around his locker, which is already covered with cards and pictures that say things like "Get Well Soon!" and "Feel Better!" and "We Miss You!"

As I move through the crowd to get to my own locker, I catch snippets of their conversations. *He sits behind me in science. My sister used to be in dance class with his sister.* Two girls are crying and hugging. It's only the second week of school. Half of these people just met the guy. Give me a break.

Jenna comes up to me and says, "Isn't it *awful*, Rory?"

She grips the straps of her backpack, which are covered with PETA and World Wildlife Fund buttons.

"I guess so," I say.

She gives me a funny look. "I mean, we don't even know how bad it is," I clarify.

Mom spent the rest of yesterday evening talking to and texting with other moms. When she came to say good night, she told me that Brent was in surgery and had a broken wrist and some other stuff. But no one really knew what was going on.

Depending on who you listen to this morning at Kensington Middle School, Brent could be (a) on life support, (b) paralyzed, or (c) missing a limb. When Danny comes down the hallway, kids swirl around him, pushing to get close.

"What happened?" someone asks.

"You were with him, right?" someone else chimes in.

"We were riding on the dirt bike path over by Addison Park, ya know?" says Danny. "When it started to get dark, we split up to ride home. The next thing I know, my mom gets a phone call and starts bawling her eyes out. She says the guy who hit him was drunk."

"Nah, I heard the driver couldn't see because it was dark, and Brent was wearing all black," someone else says.

"Is it true his leg bone was sticking out?" a girl pipes up.

"Was blood really coming out his ear?" a guy from my homeroom asks.

"Did he have a helmet on?" another girl wants to know.

The bell rings, and I push past the clump of kids. I don't want to hear any more about it.

But the first thing Mrs. Nash does is bring it up.

"Listen, I know many of you are upset about Brent's accident. Mr. Perkins has asked we not talk specifics, but . . ." She makes a fist and presses it against her lips.

"You kids need to understand that wearing a bike helmet is not optional. There is a reason your parents get on you about this!" Her voice is all wobbly and gets louder with each word. She fiddles with the charm on her necklace and clears her throat. Then she lets us do silent reading for the rest of class.

None of my other teachers mentions Brent, but between classes there is a lot of buzz. No matter where I go, his name keeps popping up like the poisonous bubbles in one of my favorite games: Marshland Attack. You have to use a blow dart to defend yourself against them. Too bad I can't use the same strategy here.

At lunch a bunch of kids are hanging out at Brent's usual table, talking in whispers. A couple of girls have paper and markers and are trying to get everyone to make cards for Brent. Even Tyson brings it up.

"Is it true you were at his house right before it happened?" he asks me.

"Yeah, with Thomas and Sunil. The moms planned it, and I had to go," I explain.

"Dude," says Tyson.

"But then he just took off on his bike?" says Jett. "Like, while people were still there?"

"Yeah. But, whatevuh," I say. "He was being obnoxious the whole time anyway."

Jenna and Melanie sit down across from us. My stomach flutters, then dips. If Jenna liked Brent before, she'll be obsessed with him now.

"I heard you were at Brent's yesterday," says Melanie.

"Why is that so fascinating to people?" My tone is a little harsher than I meant.

"Just curious if you had any privileged information." She tugs on her braids and looks down. I can see her lips whisper-spelling *privileged*, and I know I've hurt her feelings. *Nice going.*

Jenna leans across the table and stares at me. "Rory. You two used to be, like, best friends. Are you still friends with him or not?"

"Not." I can't take any more interrogation. Time to force-quit this conversation.

I get up and weave my way out of the cafeteria. Words like *bike, helicopter, hospital* hang in the air, mixing with the smells from the garbage cans. I know I'm supposed to feel bad about what happened. But I don't. I can't join in a circle with the other kids, crying and holding a candle. I won't.

Today is Wednesday, which means I have study hall instead of speech. But when I walk into the room and see Danny practically holding a press conference, some Cassius Clay–level butterflies invade my stomach. I turn around and head down to Mr. Simms's room.

"Hey." He glances at his wall calendar.

"I know it's not a speech day. But can I come in? I won't make a sound."

He tilts his head down and lifts his eyes to look at me. "Something you want to tell me?"

"It's too loud in my study hall."

He presses his hands together, tapping his pointer fingers. After a pause he lets out a long whoosh of air through pursed lips, like someone learning to whistle.

"Okay. But take this to . . . Who do you have for study hall?" he asks.

"Mrs. Sullivan."

"Take this to her so you don't get marked absent."

He scribbles on a piece of paper, folds it, and hands it to me. I know I shouldn't, but I peek at it as I walk down the hall.

It says: *Rory Mitchell will report to the speech room for fourth period until further notice.*

When I get back, I pull out my music notebook. I can hear the sound behind each mark I make on the staff paper, and I stack more and more notes on top of each other, crowding them into powerful chords. I press down hard with my pencil, trying to express how noisy it is in my mind. Mr. Simms is on his computer. The two of us work silently side by side. I look up when I hear the M&M's bag. Mr. Simms takes a handful and angles the bag toward me.

"So, how well do you know this Brent Milliken kid?" he asks.

"I don't want to talk about him," I reply.

"Oh. I thought . . . He went to your elementary school, right? I was wondering if you two were friends."

"No," I say, a little too loudly. "I mean, we used to be, but not now."

He obviously doesn't realize Brent was one of the kids in the hallway that day, and I'm too embarrassed to bring it up. *Yeah, he was with that group that was bothering me when you had to come out and save me on the first day of school.*

"Sounds complicated." He looks over at me.

I shrug.

"Fair enough." Mr. Simms reaches into the top drawer of his desk. He hands me a red marker and a sheet of paper with a block-printed *R*.

"Color this in," he says.

"Just fill it in?"

"Yup."

It's like I'm back in my old speech room, doing second-grade work. Maybe he thinks I can't handle sixth-grade stuff anymore. As I color, he pulls a dartboard out of a big crinkly shopping bag and hangs it on the back of his door. When I'm done with the *R*, he tapes it over the bull's-eye and hands me a magnetic dart.

"Go for it," he says.

I pinch the cold metal between my fingertips and pull my arm back. My muscles are loaded with all the anger I've felt for the past two days, so I let it fly with a grunt. The dart hits the top curved part of the *R*. Good.

I spend the rest of the time throwing darts at the *R*. The paper starts to rip. I'm throwing them that fast. *Thwoop.* Stupid *R*. *Thwoop.* Red, robot, reject, regret. *Thwoop.* Total loser. *Thwoop.* Screeching brakes. *Thwoop.* Hospital.

My arm starts to get tired, but I don't stop until the bell rings. Mr. Simms looks up from his laptop and nods goodbye. Neither of us has spoken for the past ten minutes. But somehow it feels like a lot's been said. Amazing how much you can communicate without using a single word.

Broken

I steady the plastic container of muffins on my lap as Mom steers around a pothole. Not that it's hard—Mom's inching the car along like she's afraid that a kid on a bike will dart out in front of her at any second.

Every year since first grade, this was the container I carried to school on my birthday, loaded with homemade whoopie pies. And every year I chose Brent to help me hand them out. If there were leftovers, we'd take them to the secretaries, and Brent would always do the talking for me. I blink away the thought.

"I hope it's enough." Mom taps the huge casserole dish on the front seat next to her.

I peek around the headrest and notice watery tomato sauce dripping onto the towel she put under the pan. "Is lasagna supposed to be soupy like that?" I ask.

"At least they'll have something for tonight." Mom leans over the steering wheel, shoulders up by her ears. "Maybe I should start one of those sign-up things. It might be a long time before things are back to normal for them. A really, really long time."

"I don't know. This feels like plenty of helping," I say.

She presses a finger against the side of her nose and takes a big inhale. Yoga breathing. Uh-oh.

"Rory. I know you were upset with Brent yesterday. But whatever is going on, I need you to set it aside. Brent's in the ICU, and his family needs our support right now." She sounds annoyed.

"ICU?" I ask.

"Intensive care unit. It's for the sickest of the sick, Rory. Brent has a huge bruise on his brain, and the doctors had to give him medicine to put him into a coma so he can sleep while the swelling goes down."

Mom's tone and the word *coma* settle on me like a cold, heavy blanket.

"So," she continues, "we'll help as much as we can for as long as they need it. Got it?"

A lady who looks like Mrs. Milliken, but shorter, answers the door at Brent's house.

"Hi, I'm Patty, one of Stephanie's friends," says Mom.

"Oh, hello," says the lady. "I'm her sister, Becky."

"I wish we weren't meeting like this," says Mom. "We're so sorry for what your family is going through."

Brent's aunt opens her mouth to say something, but then she starts to cry. Mom puts the leaky casserole dish on top of my load and gives her a hug. I take a step back and wish I could go hide in the bushes again.

Maggie comes into the open doorway and stares at me. My hands are full, so I wiggle my eyebrows and cross my eyes to try to get her to smile. Instead she pulls the top edge of her shirt up and grips the soggy collar with her teeth.

When the two ladies stop hugging, Mom says, "Becky, this is my son, Rory."

Aunt Becky turns to me and says, "Thank you both for coming." I nod and hold out the food.

As Mom explains how to heat up the lasagna, I wander off the front porch and head back toward the car. The broken pieces of the robot are still next to the driveway. I pick up one of the pipe cleaners and twist it around my finger. Over and over in my head, I hear Brent saying, *More like trying not to find him, wight?* I tighten the pipe cleaner until my fingertip starts to throb. I said I never wanted to see him again, but I didn't mean like this. I slip off the coil and fling it to the ground.

"That toy is broken," says Maggie, coming up behind me and making me jump.

"Oh, uh, yeah. Guess it is." I look down at her.

Maggie scoops up two more pipe cleaners and hands one to me.

"You can keep it," she says. She winds the other onto her wrist. "My brother is broken too."

Her parents have probably been camped out at the hospital since Brent got hurt. Her aunt is crying, and here we are bringing food. This must all be super confusing and scary for a five-year-old.

"It'll be okay. They'll fix him," I say, not knowing if it's true.

We walk across her front yard together, and I stand up the garden gnome I kicked over yesterday. I pat him on the head, and Maggie copies me.

Mom calls that it's time to go.

Maggie's big, sad eyes follow me as I slide back into the car. I force myself to smile at her and not look away. She blinks slowly and holds her hand straight up in a frozen wave.

That night Dad brings home Chinese takeout, and we eat in front of the TV, which only happens if he and Mom are both super tired. When we're done, Dad clears our plates and then scoots next to me on the couch and scratches my back, something he hasn't done in forever. I lean into his hand.

I glance at the clock and notice it's getting really late, but no one says anything about bedtime. Mom covers the three of us with a blanket, and I snuggle in instead of squirming away like I usually do. I sit there between them, and it feels really safe and really good. Tonight, I don't want space.

Someone New

The next week in math, Mrs. Lucas tells us to get into groups for a hands-on project. I hate working in groups. It means having to talk.

Jenna grabs my arm. "Come with me, Rory."

I smile and follow her. Okay, not *all* groups. She leads me over to a girl who is wearing black boots, polka-dot leggings, and a flannel shirt. I had noticed her before because she likes to raise her hand and answer questions in class. But I didn't know Jenna knew her.

"Asha, want to group up with me and Rory?" Jenna asks the girl.

"Sure!" she replies. "But I wish we were back at the pool club instead of here!"

"Ditto," says Jenna.

Asha smiles at me, and I nod. My plan is to stay quiet and follow along.

"Okay, listen up," says Mrs. Lucas. "Welcome to the metric system! Staying in this room or the hallway outside, I want you to estimate and measure the items listed on this paper. Choose one person to hold the meter stick and one to hold the clipboard and record the results for your group."

Asha grabs the clipboard, and Jenna hands me the meter stick. "No air guitar, Rory," she says.

"Who, me?" I ask.

"Rory's totally into guitar, Asha. He's *really* good. He played in the show at the end of music and arts camp, and he had a solo and everything."

Jenna had taken the dramatic-flair class at camp, and her monologue from the point of view of a captive dolphin had gotten a standing ovation.

"I'm not that gweat," I say, and immediately regret it. I forgot to check for *r* sounds.

But Asha says, "Cool. I can't even play the triangle."

"Please begin," says Mrs. Lucas.

We measure a bunch of things around the classroom, like the bin we put our homework in, a calculator, and the big storage cubbies along the side wall. Asha is like Jenna—she never asks me to repeat myself. I start to relax a little. When we head out to the hallway to measure one of the bulletin boards, we switch jobs. Now I have the clipboard while Jenna measures.

"Can you believe it about that kid who got hit by the car?" asks Asha. She pulls her long wavy hair up behind her head and sticks a pencil in to hold it there.

"Brent Milliken," Jenna says, looking at me. "We went to elementary school with him."

"They're saying he's got a brain injury and is in a coma," Asha whispers. "Like, not waking up."

"I heard that too," says Jenna. "It's so, so sad."

"I know a kid whose uncle died from something like that," Asha whispers.

Jenna's eyes widen. She nibbles on a fingernail.

I get that the way they look—mopey and scared—is the appropriate emotion here. This is serious stuff. But the part of me that's still mad at Brent is like a force field blocking my ability to feel sympathy. Except it only works on Brent, because I can't stand seeing the girls so sad right now.

"He'll be okay," I say, even though I have no clue if that's true. "My mom said he's in the coma because they gave him medicine to keep him asleep."

"What?" asks Asha. "I didn't even know that was a thing."

"What are you *girls* talking about?" A snarky voice behind me juts into our conversation.

I turn and see Danny, swinging a wooden hall pass by its leather strap. What is the deal with this guy? He's like a piece of stepped-on gum, the kind that wedges into the treads of your shoe so you can never fully get rid of it. Can't I go one class period without seeing him?

"Nothing," I say. My fingers tighten on the clipboard.

"Nothing?" He steps closer. "Figures. No one can understand your baby talk, anyway."

He hits the bottom of the clipboard and sends it flying. "Oops," he says, and walks away.

I'm tempted to show him some sign language I *know* he'd understand, but I don't want to be rude in front of the girls, so I jam my hands into my pockets instead. I feel a sharp stab as the wire from the middle of the pipe cleaner Maggie handed me scrapes along my thumb. I had forgotten it was in there. *Robot, reject, regret.*

"What's his deal?" says Asha, handing me back the clipboard.

"He was the one riding bikes with Brent right before Brent got hit," says Jenna.

"So that gives him the right to be a jerk?" asks Asha.

"It doesn't. I was just saying," says Jenna.

"I think being nasty is kind of his specialty," I say.

I get an urge again to share the dirt on Danny's mom. But I decide I'm not gonna be like Brent, spilling information after I promised not to.

"Forget about him, Rory," says Jenna.

I wish I could. There are a lot of things I wish I could forget.

Operation Taffy

When I get to speech, the door is locked and the room is dark. I sit down on the scratchy hallway carpeting to wait. The cut on my thumb is a thin red line, and it stings. I turn my hand over and trace the scar on my palm from a much bigger injury. Brent and I were playing in the woods behind my house when I fell onto a sharp stick poking up from the ground. I started bawling and freaking out when I saw all the blood. Brent pressed his shirt against the cut, made me laugh with a joke about stinky armpits, and helped me get home. I think he had to throw that shirt away.

"Been waiting long?" asks Mr. Simms, walking up and unlocking the door.

"Nope." I follow him into the room, hoping for another silent session. But he has other plans.

"So, how are things going, Rory?" he asks as I slide into my chair. "Settling in and making some new friends?"

"I guess," I say, thinking of Asha.

"C'mon, got any details for me? What's the real 411 at Kensington Middle?"

"Lately it seems like all anyone can talk about is what happened to Bwent," I say.

"Well, that's understandable." Mr. Simms nods.

"It's kind of annoying, though," I say.

"Oh? How so?"

"Because people act like he's a saint. Like he's the best guy in the whole school. But he's not. He's actually kind of mean," I say.

Mr. Simms leans in. "In what way?"

I don't feel like explaining the whole big thing. "He just is."

"Hmm." He waits for me to add more, but I stay quiet.

"Well, no one's perfect," he continues. "I'm sure you agree. But when something big happens to someone, people tend to forget the 'not great' parts about them. Muhammad Ali is a national hero, right? But tell that to the several wives he left for other women, huh?"

I raise my eyebrows.

Mr. Simms claps his hands and rubs them together. "Speaking of Ali, have you been working on your rhyme?"

"Yeah, but it's all still *w*'s," I say.

"Okay," he says. "Time for Operation Taffy."

"Huh?"

Mr. Simms opens his desk drawer, pushes aside the M&M's, and pulls out a small bag of taffy. Willy Wonka would love this guy.

"Pick your flavor," he says. I choose grape.

Mr. Simms puts on plastic gloves like the school nurse uses and sets a tongue depressor out on a stack of paper towels. I lean back from him a little and press my lips together.

"What's with the gloves?" I mumble out the side of my mouth.

"It's nothing bad!" he promises. "Just have to get a little up-close with your molars." He unwraps the taffy and starts cutting it into thin slivers with a plastic knife.

"Okay, bear with me," he says, rolling a piece of taffy between his thumb and forefinger. He hands me a mirror. "I'm going to put this right where I want your tongue to go. That way you can see and feel exactly what the target is. All right?"

"I like candy," I say, shrugging.

"Same. Now open wide."

I watch in the mirror as he carefully sticks a small strip of taffy on the inside of my upper teeth toward the back of my mouth, first on the right, and then on the left.

"Okay, Rory, those are your targets. And these"—he taps the sides of my tongue with the depressor—"are your darts. Press the darts against the targets and your muscles will be exactly where they need to be to make the *r* sound. Try *ree*."

My tongue fights me as I struggle to force it into position. I can taste the grape taffy, and I have to suck in the drool. I swallow, then try again. I take a deep breath, push hard.

"Ree," I say. "Ree? Ree!"

"Yes!" Mr. Simms's fist pumps the air. "How does that feel?"

"Wet." I wipe my mouth with a paper towel.

"Ree," I say again, grinning. I try my name.

"Wohwy." Dang it.

"Ree," I say, slowly and with effort.

And then again, "Wohwy."

The candy slips, and I swallow it. Then I make a face in the mirror.

"This is tough." I want my name to come out the way *ree* did.

Mr. Simms pops a piece of taffy in his mouth and talks around it. "Think of it this way: Your tongue has been sunbathing, making that sound the same way in that same word for eleven years. Now we're asking it to be a surfer, to stand up and be strong. You'll get there. One syllable at a time. You've got this, Rory."

He hands me another index card. "Put this with the other one."

I read it. *My face is so pretty, you don't see a scar, which proves I'm the king of the ring by far.* It's an *r* minefield. "Did you make this up?"

Mr. Simms shakes his head and smiles. "It's from a song about Ali called 'Black Superman.' Now try saying *ring.*"

"Wing." Ugh.

"Try again. Start with a growl. *Grrr . . . ing.* Slowly."

I reposition my tongue, imagine the taffy. "*Grrr . . .* ing. *Grrr*ing. *Rrring.*"

Mr. Simms grabs my forearm and lifts it up. "Ladies and gentlemen, today's winner in a ninth-round knockout, the Lakeville Lip!"

I float out of there, riding the crest of an epic wave of happiness.

Lockdown

When the wave crashes on me the following weekend, it hits hard.

"I'm not going in." I grip the car door handle with both hands.

"Yes, you are," says Mom. "We'll be quick—I promise."

She comes around to my side and stands with her arms crossed. She'll wait there all day, I know. So after about a minute, I give up. I slide out and turtle into my coat, breathing my own warm air. I follow the click of Mom's shoes down the grimy stairwell of the hospital parking garage.

"Brent's finally out of the ICU, and it's really important to Mrs. Milliken that he have some visitors. But I want you to be prepared that he probably still has some tubes and medical equipment attached to him. And he gets overwhelmed easily, so let's speak quietly and keep things low-key." She turns to look at me.

"So no jam session, then?"

"Not funny, Rory."

I know it's not. None of this is funny.

When the elevator opens on the eighth floor, I immediately smell a mixture of scrambled eggs and the boys' bathroom from school.

In front of us are two big metal doors, closed tight. One is decorated with a faded paper scarecrow, with his arms and legs hanging straight down from his body, the fasteners loose. The other has a keypad on it labeled *Nurses' Station*. Mom presses the red call button.

"Yes?" a voice answers.

"We're here to see Brent Milliken," says Mom.

"How many people?"

"Two."

"Come on in."

A harsh buzzer sounds, and the doors swing open toward us.

"What's with the lockdown?" I whisper.

"Mrs. Milliken said this is a special secure floor for people with brain injuries. The doors are locked for the patients' safety," says Mom.

The first thing I see is a group of people wearing helmets and sitting in wheelchairs. They're in a small open area near some windows, off to the side of what looks like a hotel check-in desk. One guy is shouting "Let me outta here!" and another is moaning. Trying not to stare, I stand close behind Mom while she signs us in.

I hear clanking metal, high-pitched beeps, and crying as we walk down the hallway. I glance into one of the rooms and see a bunch of people holding hands around someone on a bed.

I grab the bottom edge of Mom's jean jacket.

Inside Brent's room it's much quieter. There are two beds. The one by the door is empty; Brent's in the one by the window. His mom pops out of her chair and waves us in.

"Oh, Patty, thanks so much for coming! And Rory," she says, pulling me into a hug.

Mrs. Milliken is wearing sweatpants and no makeup, which seems weird because she usually dresses like she's about to go out to a fancy restaurant. I stand straight and frozen, my eyes on Brent.

"Brent, honey," she says, "the Mitchells are here."

I don't even recognize him. His eyes are closed, and his face is swollen. Half of his hair is shaved, and there are strips of staples, like a ladder, holding together a huge cut on the right side of his head. There's a bulky bandage around his left wrist and hand. Next to him is a big machine with a display that looks like something you'd see in the cockpit of a plane. Lights are blinking, and numbers keep changing and flashing.

Another machine makes a steady, loud whirring noise. There is a tube attached to it, and I follow it with my eyes to where it connects to Brent, right through a hole in the bottom part of his neck. The tube makes a crackling sound, and the oatmeal I ate for breakfast threatens a nasty return.

"Hi, Brent," whispers Mom. "We hope you feel better soon."

Brent does not move.

"I'm sorry he's asleep right now," says Mrs. Milliken. "He's off the heavy sedatives, but he still gets tired very easily."

She leans over and takes his unbandaged hand, which I now see is actually tied to the bed. Mrs. Milliken sees me staring.

"Brent was getting a little feisty and was trying to pull out his breathing tube," she explains. "You don't like that thing, do you, troublemaker?" she asks Brent as she adjusts his pillow.

She taps a section of the tubing on his chest and looks up at Mom. "In the ICU the tube went in through his mouth. This smaller tube is a step in the right direction. But he still can't say anything." Her face crumples.

Mom puts an arm around her, and they walk to the window, chatting in whispers.

I stand near Brent's feet and tie my fleece around my waist. It's like a hundred degrees in here. I cross my arms so I don't accidentally touch anything. Everything seems sad—the machines, the metal side rails on the bed, the empty bulletin board. Then I notice Mr. Bear-Bear propped on a small side table, right out in the open. I can't believe it. Brent teases other kids about stuffed animals all the time, even though he never stopped hiding Mr. Bear-Bear in his sleeping bag during sleepovers. But I'm the only one who knows that. Well, I *was* the only one, until . . . I squeeze my eyes shut.

When I open them, I look right at Brent. "Is he going to be okay?"

The moms turn from the window and come back over. Mom grabs my hand, and Mrs. Milliken gives me a big, odd smile that reminds me of the nurse at my doctor's office—the one who gives the shots.

"Yes," she says. "He's going to be just fine, and having visits from friends is good medicine, for sure. You're the first, Rory. Thank you for coming."

But I'm *not* his friend. He doesn't want me to be. And speaking of that, why am I the only one here? The guys he's friends with at school should be visiting, not me. I keep those thoughts to myself and glance at the clock. Didn't Mom say this would be quick?

Suddenly the machine with the blinking lights makes a *whomp-whomp-whomp* noise. Mom pulls me back against the wall as two nurses rush in.

"Who's making all that noise?" one says gently as he pushes a button to silence the alarm. The other nurse fiddles with the breathing tube.

"He needs to be suctioned," that nurse says. "Pull the curtain."

But before it slides closed, I see her unhook the tube at Brent's neck and jab a sucker thing like the dentist uses into the hole in his throat. He starts gagging and coughing, and this time I really do have to puke. I press my hand to my lips and look frantically at Mom. She whisks me into a small bathroom out in the hall.

Mom stays and rubs my back, then wets a rough paper towel and puts it on my neck. "I'm sorry. I'm sorry," she says.

When I'm done, I stand up and move over to the sink to rinse my mouth.

"I'll wait outside," Mom says.

I swish and spit, then splash water on my face. In the old, cloudy mirror, I'm an unsettling mix of gray and yellow. There's no way I'm going back in that room. I wait in the hallway and listen as Mom says goodbye to Mrs. Milliken and Brent and promises to visit again soon. She can if she wants. But this place is way too depressing. I'm never coming back here.

When we get home, I go straight to my room and pick up my guitar. I slowly pluck the main riff of "The Unforgiven," track four on the album Mr. Simms told me about. I put on the song and play it over and over, trying to figure out the notes. But no matter how much I focus, I can't stop hearing and smelling Brent's hospital room.

The day has warmed up, so I open my window to let in some fresh air. Mr. Garland is trimming the bushes in his side yard. I plug into the amp and turn it up so he can hear. I keep practicing the line until I can do it without any pauses. When I look out again, Mr. Garland is standing still, his face tilted up, listening.

After a while I stop playing and sit down at my desk. I twist the guitar strap tight around my wrist, remembering the thick piece of fabric tying Brent to his bed. Brent was the one who got on his bike and rode off. No one made him do that or any of the other awful stuff he's done to me. So why should I care if he's hurting now?

I let the strap go, and my numb hand wakes up with prickly tingles as the blood rushes back. Not my friend, not my problem.

The One-Two Punch

Danny comes up to me in language arts on Monday and stands over my desk. I try to ignore him.

"Heard you went and visited Milliken," he says.

"Who told you that?" He can't seriously have a problem with this. I pick at the edge of my binder.

"My dad. He called to see if he could go visit, since he's the wrestling coach and all. But they said it wasn't a good idea, because you'd already been there, and Brent needed to rest. Nice going. You probably made him worse." He kicks the back leg of my chair as he walks away.

The final bell rings, and Mrs. Nash clears her throat. "As many of you with older siblings already know, one of the biggest assignments of your sixth-grade year is the biography project."

Some kids moan, but one guy hoots.

"It accounts for thirty percent of your grade in language arts," she says in a louder voice, her stare shutting down the noise as she drops stacks of stapled packets on the first desk in each row.

"Pass them back," she instructs. The flutter of papers sounds like a flock of birds taking off.

"You are middle schoolers now. And this project is designed to prepare you for the term papers you'll tackle in high school. This is not something you're going to whip up in one weekend. It'll be an ongoing assignment, and I'll help you break it up into manageable chunks. We'll start slow, focusing first on research techniques and digital-literacy skills. Next semester I'll guide you through the process of analyzing and synthesizing your data. Your work will culminate in April, when you'll present your final project in front of the entire sixth grade."

She keeps talking, but I stop listening after "in front of the entire sixth grade." There is no way. Small humiliations are hard enough to deal with. But another giant public one? No thanks. How could Mr. Simms not have mentioned this when he saw how freaked out I was about Step-Up Day?

"Rory. *Rory!*" Melanie passes over the extra packet from her row. I zone back in and take the assignment by the corners, holding it away from me.

"For this project," Mrs. Nash continues, "you will choose a public figure—alive or dead—who you think has made an impact on our society. I call this a 'project of tens.' You must use a minimum of ten sources, you'll turn in ten images of your subject with full-paragraph descriptions, and the oral portion must be ten minutes long."

The air around me seems to fill with water. Mrs. Nash's voice goes blurry, and so do the words on the page in front of me. I can't breathe. I'm sinking.

Kids chatter around me.

Mrs. Nash holds up her hand. "I understand that this is a huge amount of work. Because of its scope, you'll work in pairs. I want you and your partner to really get to know the person you choose to study, and your project should make us feel as if we know them as well."

Immediately people look at each other and point or nod, silently forming pairs. Melanie catches my eye, and I smile. What could be better than a partner who already knows practically all the words in the English language? This will be P-E-R-F-E-C-T.

"Before you go choosing a partner," says Mrs. Nash, "don't."

Kids freeze, and one girl says, "What?"

"Middle school is also about meeting new people," Mrs. Nash says.

I drop my head. I do *not* need to be reminded about that.

"I'll pull names out of this basket." She shakes the strips of paper inside. "When you're called, gather your things and stand along the side of the room. After everyone has a partner, I want you to sit back down next to each other. That will be your seat for the rest of the year."

She begins picking names. Some kids smile and fist-bump. Others stand next to each other awkwardly. I press my arms close to my sides. I'm hoping my partner is the talkative type. Because I'm not doing any of the presentation part.

"Rory Mitchell and Brent Milliken," reads Mrs. Nash. The room hushes.

Mrs. Nash purses her lips. She makes a quiet clicking noise with her tongue. I look over at Brent's empty desk and grip my pencil, hoping she'll skip over him and give me a different partner.

"We're hoping Brent will be back with us after winter break. You'll start the research on your own, Rory, and Brent will join in as soon as he's well enough." She folds our names together like it's settled.

"The important thing is you'll each be able to tackle your own half of the oral presentation," she adds.

Ouch! It's a stunning one-two punch to our boy Mitchell!

"Did everyone hear that? The oral portion needs to be split fifty-fifty. I make it a priority that all my students gain public speaking experience." She goes back to pairing up kids.

I start to stand up with the rest of the class and then realize there's no point. I'm like that guy at the hospital who was shouting "Let me outta here!" Nervous, mad, and totally stuck.

Muscle Memory

As soon as I get to the speech room, I collapse into a chair and rest my chin on the table. Mr. Simms flips the page of the book he's reading and spreads it upside down on his desk. I see the words *Brain Injury*.

"Tired today? Me too." He rubs his fingers on his scalp, which makes his floppy hair look all bushy and wild.

"Did you know about this ten-minute bio thing we have to do?" I sit back and hold my fingers up. Ten.

"Ah, the big biography project. You're starting that already?" he asks.

"Yeah. *I* am, on my own. Why didn't you tell me about it?"

"I didn't want to overwhelm you. It seems like maybe public speaking isn't your favorite."

"You think?" I cover my face.

"Wait, back up a sec, though. What do you mean, on your own? I thought everyone got a partner," he says.

"Everyone else did." I stare at his book. "I got Bwent. Mrs. Nash says he'll be back and can 'join in.'"

"Hmm, okay," he says. "How do you feel about that?"

I scan for *r*'s before I answer. *Terrible. Miserable.*

"Bad," I say.

Things were weird enough between us before his accident. What will they be like now? What will *he* be like? I picture him in his hospital room.

"Will he even be able to do anything?" I ask.

"Recovery from a brain injury is different for everyone," Mr. Simms says. "There's so much involved. Memory, language, speech, thinking. Not to mention all the motor skills he may have to relearn. There's no way to predict how much time Brent will need. So let's assume you might have to do this project on your own. Would that be the end of the world?"

"Yes!" I say. "I'd have to talk for ten minutes! I can't stop and put taffy in my mouth each time I have to say something. And why is my own name still so impossible? Why can I say *ree* on its own, but not *woh*? And why can't I say the *ree* when it's in my name? What's up with that?"

"I'll answer you, but can we be happy for one second that you just said *ree* without thinking about it? And without any taffy or tricks?" Mr. Simms smiles at me.

"No," I say. Then I smile too. "Fine. One second."

"Here's what's going on, Rory."

He pulls out a blank piece of paper and draws the side view of a head with a wide-open mouth and a snakelike tongue.

"The tongue is a great muscle—eight muscles, actually. But in a way, it's lazy. It wants to move the least amount it needs to. And if a bunch of sounds are squished together in one word, it really has to work hard and move around a lot, which yours hates. You follow?"

"Sunbathing. Lazy."

"Right. Your tongue wants to relax as it heads to the *oh.* So it slips out of the *r* position easily. But when you say *ee,* your tongue is high in your mouth, and your lips are pulled back. The tongue stays in a better position for the *r* in that case."

I'm trying to pay attention, but high, back, what? This is confusing.

Mr. Simms looks at me and stands up. "Come on. Field trip."

I follow him down the quiet hallway toward the gym. Thankfully there's no sound coming from inside. Mr. Simms is cool and all, but it's not like I want to be seen getting extra help.

We walk across the empty basketball court.

"See this semicircle?" asks Mr. Simms. "The three-point line."

"Yup. My dad taught me," I say.

"Right. Okay. So let's pretend the three-point line is the inside of your mouth." He walks to the middle of the arc. "Your tonsils are back here." Then he points toward the basket. "Over there is where your mouth opens."

"The baseline is my lips," I say.

"Exactly. And we are your tongue." He motions for me to come stand next to him.

"We're my tongue?" I laugh a little.

"Yes! And as I was saying, your tongue moves around in your mouth, changing positions depending on the sound you're making. The way a basketball player moves around the court." He grabs an orange cone and puts it a few feet to the left along the three-point line.

"That's the taffy target. Your tongue hangs out there for both the *r* sound and *ee.* When those two sounds are next to each other, your tongue doesn't have to move very much. That makes it happy. That's why it's easier."

"My tongue has feelings?" I say, smiling. I'm actually starting to get what he is saying.

"Now, when you say *oh*, your tongue moves down here." He takes another orange cone and sets it a few feet to the right of me on the line.

"This is the bottom of your mouth. So, when an *r* sound is next to an *oh*, it has to move from there"—he points to the first cone— "all the way down to where I'm standing now."

"Lazy tongue. Not happy," I say.

"Bingo! Okay, come stand here at this cone. This is *ro*."

I take his spot while he goes to grab a basketball.

He tosses it to me. "Say *ro*."

"Wo."

"Growl first. Grrrrr . . . ro," he demonstrates.

"Grrrr . . . wro." Ugh. "Grrrr . . . ro!" Yes!

"Nice! Pass me the ball. Now run up to the other cone," he instructs me.

I jog over and stop.

"That's *ree*." He bounces the ball to me. "Say it."

"Ree."

"Yes! Back to *ro*," he says.

I toss the ball to him and run back.

I keep going back and forth: *ro, ree, ro, ree, ro, ree*. On the next catch, I keep the ball and rush forward, dodging Mr. Simms and sinking a layup.

"Do you know what muscle memory is?" asks Mr. Simms, grabbing the ball on the second bounce.

I shake my head.

"It's why great athletes are so consistent. Great musicians too. They do the same thing over and over and over, training their muscles exactly what to do to make the basket or to hit the right note." He dribbles the ball.

"Like Muhammad Ali—his muscles knew how to tense, jab, and dodge practically before his brain sent the signals. And when you learn a song on the guitar—it's not easy at first, right? But once you practice a ton, your fingers seem to know what to do." Mr. Simms passes the ball to me, and I nod.

"Well, your tongue is a muscle, and we need to retrain its memory," he says. "Pretty soon you won't need the taffy, and you won't need to stop and think about the *r* sound. Your muscles will remember. Like they did with that layup. You've obviously done that before."

I dribble the ball, and my mind flashes to Brent and me passing a basketball back and forth at his house. *Show me how to do that,* I'd asked him after watching him do a layup. He went through the steps in slow motion, letting me try over and over until I got it. He was always the better player, but whenever we went one-on-one, he'd pretend to make mistakes if he got too far ahead so the game would last longer. Or maybe—maybe—he was being nice.

"What about Bwent's muscles?" I ask, stopping the ball.

"Well, I hope they have an excellent memory. It helps that he's a young, athletic guy. But many things will be hard for him at first. You both have a lot of practicing ahead of you. Luckily *pra*ctice makes *per*fect. Ooh! Consonant clusters—that's a whole 'nother thing to look forward to!" Mr. Simms grabs the ball from me.

"What?"

"Don't worry about that today. Let's save those for later."

We spend the rest of the time playing one-on-one. As I move around the court, I hear chord progressions in my mind. The music is pulsing and fast, the best kind of heavy. The tune crescendos and peaks when I land a game-winning rimless shot.

This is my kind of speech therapy.

Rehab

The next morning we get an unexpected school delay. The temperature dipped last night, freezing the rain into a slick, icy shell that covers everything. Mom and I are picking through our box of Halloween decorations when the phone rings. She stands up and cradles it against her ear as she unwinds a string of orange and purple lights.

"Hello? . . . Stephanie! I've been thinking about you!" she says into the phone.

Brent's mom. I put down the foam leg bone of the skeleton I'm piecing together.

"Oh, that's fantastic. I'm so happy for you guys." Pause. "Of course, we'd love to come visit!"

Visit? I pull my *Scream* mask from the box and slip it on.

"Great news!" Mom says after she hangs up. "Brent is doing so well, they're moving him to a rehab facility! Hopefully he'll be back home in time for Christmas!"

I push the mask up off my face. "Isn't that the kind of place that addicts go?"

"Not that kind of rehab. Salmon Brook specializes in helping people with brain injuries. Mrs. Milliken wants us to come visit once he's settled in." She gives me a look.

The blood rushes out of my head.

"Don't worry," says Mom. "No tubes this time, and no monitors. He's much better. You'll see."

"Can he talk now?" I ask.

"Yes. His breathing tube is out, and he's finally alert enough to follow simple conversations."

"Then I don't know if he'd want me to visit," I say.

"What? Are you still thinking about him riding off that day?" she asks. "Please tell me that after all this, you can forgive him for that. Brent is one of your oldest friends. He needs your support."

Was one of my oldest friends.

"Mom, Bwent is—"

"Brent," she says, cutting me off, "is a boy struggling to recover from a devastating injury. Think about how you'd feel if you were in his position."

I *don't* want to think about that. And I don't want to think about before he got hurt either. I don't want to think about anything. I wish there were a way to turn off my brain. Which is a horrible thing to want when that's sort of what happened to someone you know.

"It's almost bus time," I say.

When I go upstairs to get my backpack, I see Mr. Garland out on his porch, spreading salt on his steps. I crack open the window, and even though I'm no Jimi Hendrix, I pick out the first few bars of "The Star-Spangled Banner" on my guitar. On my way down the street, Mr. Garland salutes me.

Later that morning Mrs. Nash announces that we'll go down to the library during class time.

"Mrs. Dailey will guide us through the biography section so you can see what resources our school has available. And then while you finish up brainstorming with your partner, I will conference with each project team. I'd like you to make your final subject selection today," she says.

Once we get a short tour of the new-to-us middle-school library, most partner pairs start talking to each other. I keep quiet, since I'd only be talking to myself.

I walk along the shelves in the biography section, tapping a few book spines with my finger. *J. S. Bach—not my speed. Thomas Edison—hmm, I turn on a light bulb, and my project is done? Alexander Hamilton—I think you've gotten enough play lately, buddy.*

"I'll start with you, Rory Mitchell." Mrs. Nash motions to me, and I sit down next to her at one of the tables.

"I know you're on your own for now, but our hope is that Brent will return at the beginning of next semester. What I'd like is for you to make a solid start on the research so he can join in when he gets back," she says as if this is new information.

I know Mom says he's gotten much better, but the last time I saw Brent, he couldn't even keep his eyes open. I can't picture the guy I saw in the hospital bed joining anything.

Mrs. Nash stands up. "Excuse me, class. We're here to work, not socialize. If you're on a computer, I want to see serious research only, please."

She sits back down and straightens her stack of paper. "Okay. Any thoughts on whom you'd like to profile?"

"Well . . ." I rub my hands on my thighs. Someone knocks a globe off a shelf in the geography section, and Mrs. Nash pinches the bridge of her nose. I'd better come up with something fast.

"It's been a whole week. Have you thought about it at all?" she asks.

"Yeah, I've thought about it," I say. I've thought about how much pain and torture this whole thing is going to be.

"And?" She taps her pen on the edge of the table and turns in her seat, shushing the class.

I click through famous people in my mind. I'm about to go with boring Edison and his kite—*he had the kite, right?*—when I shove my hand in my pocket and feel the index cards Mr. Simms has me carrying around. *Yes.*

"Can it be an athlete?" I ask.

"Athletes often make a significant impact on our society," she says, nodding. "Anyone specific?"

"Muhammad Ali."

She sits back and smiles. "That could work. What do you know about him?"

"Um, he was awesome at boxing. He was the heavyweight champion," I say.

"Anything else?" she asks.

"I know he changed his name, but that's about all," I admit.

"That's okay—it just means you have a lot to learn. There's quite a bit more to him than boxing. I think he's an excellent subject for your biography project. I approve."

She writes *Muhammad Ali* and her initials on the top of my assignment sheet.

"There's a wealth of information about him online. But I'd like you to start by seeing what you can find in terms of print materials," she says.

"Okay," I say. A tiny bit of air gets pumped into my deflated attitude. I know exactly where to go.

Loser Land

"**A**sha, over here!" calls Jenna from the table where we're all eating.

Jenna and Melanie almost always sit with us at lunch now. Tyson is flipping a pencil with one hand, grabbing chips with the other, and quizzing Melanie from her new *Champion Spellers* book. She's hoping to be the schoolwide winner again, but she's nervous about competing against seventh and eighth graders for the first time.

"What's up, people?" says Asha, climbing onto the bench next to me. We move our trays to make room for her.

"I'm helping Melanie *assuage* her fears about the upcoming spelling bee," says Tyson.

"Very good!" Melanie smiles at him.

"I told you—not just a pretty face," Tyson says, pointing at himself.

"Ugh, someone change the subject, quick," says Jett.

"Ooh, did you guys hear?" asks Asha. "That kid Brent is getting out of the hospital."

"Yeah," I say. "But he's not coming home yet. My mom told me he moved to a new place. She's gonna make me visit him again."

"You're going to see him *again*?" asks Tyson. "What's up with that?"

"You know my mom. Mrs. Milliken asked us to. It's not like I want to go."

Jett pulls his camouflage ranger cap down over his eyebrows and nods for me to turn around. Danny is in full bulky cornstalk mode, looming over me. His crew of guys is with him. *Scrape off, you stupid wad of gum!*

"What are you saying about Milliken?" Danny asks.

I don't answer.

"Rory said Brent's moved from the hospital to somewhere else," says Jenna. "His mom is asking people to come visit."

"Why would he want you dorks to visit?" Danny spits out.

"Maybe he's lonely, *Sherry*," says Tyson. "How many times have you been to see him?"

That shuts him up. But a second later, something cold and wet trickles between my shoulder blades and down my back.

"What the heck?" I spin around and see Danny holding a carton of milk.

"Yeah, watch it, dude," Danny says to the kid next to him. "You shoved me and look what happened!"

"No, I didn't!" The kid takes a step back, shaking his head.

"Well, then it looks like Baby Wohwy spilled his milky." Danny laughs.

Tyson stands up and takes a step toward Danny. Jenna grabs Tyson's arm, and Melanie pulls her book to her chest and curls around it.

"Just get out of here, Danny," says Jett. "Leave us alone."

One of the lunch monitors starts walking toward us.

"I wouldn't want to stay here in Loser Land, anyway," Danny says.

"Look who's talking," I say. My voice is shaking.

Danny starts to laugh. Tyson clenches his fists.

"What*evah*, Wohwy," says Danny. He glares at us, then turns and walks away.

I arch my back away from my soggy shirt.

"Are you okay?" Jenna asks me.

"Fine." I pull my shirt around and dab at it with a stack of cruddy cafeteria napkins.

"Talk about Sergeant Major Jerk," says Jett.

"Dude has issues," says Asha.

"Everything okay over here?" asks the lunch monitor.

"Yup, all good!" I say, twisting so she can't see my back.

"All right, carry on," she says, continuing her loop around the room.

"You sure you're all right?" Asha asks when the monitor is far enough away.

"Totally fine. I'm gonna go change," I say, thinking of the long-sleeve layer I left in my locker yesterday.

As I walk toward the exit, it feels like every single person in the cafeteria is staring at my back. Like there's a neon sign flashing three words: *baby, loser, reject.*

Mithter Thimth

"**W**hat's this?" asks Mr. Simms.

He finds me standing at the sink in the speech room, rinsing my T-shirt. The door was unlocked, and I figured this would be way less embarrassing than trying to do it in the boys' bathroom.

"I spilled something at lunch," I explain, pushing up my long sleeves.

"Musta been quite a spill. Here, let me." He takes the shirt and wrings it out.

I go over to his bookshelf and turn my head to the side to read the titles. He searches his desk drawer, pulls out a plastic bag, drops my shirt in, and ties it shut.

"Have a seat," he says.

We sit across from each other at the table. He holds up the bag. "You wanna tell me about this?"

"Nothing to tell. I'm just clumsy." I look at him sideways.

He raises his eyebrows.

"Weally!"

"*Really?*"

I stop and concentrate. Tongue back. Sides pushed against teeth. Big breath. Tense muscles. "Rrrweally."

"Nice!" he says. "That was a great *r*, but are you sure everything's cool?"

"Yup. Like I said, just an accident."

He stares at me. I study the tabletop, then glance up at him and shrug.

"All right, all right," he says. "Down to business, then. How's the biography project going? Who'd you pick to study?"

"Guess." I point to his bookshelf.

"You chose my man Muhammad?" He pushes his chair back and bounces on the balls of his feet, throwing jabs at an invisible punching bag.

"Yeah. Mrs. Nash signed off on it. I was hoping I could use some of these books?"

"Of course! I'm happy to help you, especially until . . . um, your partner gets back. And we'll practice the oral presentation as part of your speech work, okay?" He sits back down.

"Yippee." I roll my eyes.

"Which part is the 'yippee' for? The partner or the presentation?" he asks.

"Both." I look right at him.

"Elaborate, please."

"It's just . . . sometimes I wish Bwent didn't go to this school. Him and some othuh kids too."

I wait for Mr. Simms to say something about acceptance, and how we should feel sorry for Brent and support him in any way we can, blah, blah, blah. But instead he leans back in his chair and squints at me with his arms crossed.

"You've mentioned before that Brent's not your favorite. What's behind that?"

I press my fingernail into the soft wood exposed by a scrape on the table's shiny surface.

"It's okay, Rory. Maybe I can help. I had a few Brents in my life when I was in middle school." Mr. Simms looks at me.

"You did?"

"I don't tell many people about this, but I'll tell you." He pauses. "Okay, you know how frustrating it is that you can't say *r*, especially because your name has two of them?"

I nod.

"Well, my letter was *s*. Came out *th* every time. Every darn time."

Hang on. Simms. *Thimth*. "Oh, my gosh, so you couldn't say Simms!"

He grins. "It gets worse. You ready for this? My first name is Steve."

"You've got to be kidding me. *Steve Simms* and you couldn't say *s*? Dude. That stinks. I mean, that *thinkth*." I crack up.

"Tell me about it! And I can't believe you're laughing at me!"

"Thowwy, I'll thtop," I say.

We both laugh then. After a while, I force my face to be serious. I pinch my lips between my teeth to make sure I don't start smiling again.

"Okay, I apologize," I say. "So, when did you finally get *s*?"

"Right around seventh grade. So, there's hope for you! Listen." He pauses and clenches his teeth together. "Ssteve Ssimmss."

I give him a thumbs-up.

"I retrained my muscles and my teeth to get in an exaggerated position each time I say an *s* sound. It worked for me, and it'll work for you too, Rory. I promi*sssssse*."

I tap my tongue against my front teeth. I'm starting to believe him. "You got teased?"

"All the time. Got called the Spitter, Baby Mouth, you name it. It was rough."

"What did you do about it?" I ask.

"Mostly I stayed as quiet as I could and kept my head down. But I regret that. I couldn't help the way I spoke. I wish I had stood up for myself more. One thing that helped was finding an adult I could talk to about my feelings. Do you talk to your parents about any of this?" he asks.

"I think they feel kinda bad about naming me what they did. I don't want to make them feel guilty," I say. "Anyway if I told my mom, she'd make it into a huge thing, and next thing you know I'd be in some self-esteem class."

"What about your dad?"

"My dad's not into feelings. He gets all stiff and goes into coach-at-halftime mode." I lower my voice to mimic Dad: "Best way to let it out is to sweat it out, son."

Mr. Simms puts a hand over his smile. "Well, you can always talk to me, okay?"

"Okay."

"Really. Let me know if anything is bothering you or if anything is getting, you know, out of hand." He shifts his eyes to the plastic bag with my wet shirt.

I nod. The bell rings.

"One more quick thing," says Mr. Simms, glancing at the clock. "I have a new rhyme for you."

He picks up an index card from his desk and reads, "'I done wrassled with an alligator, I done tussled with a whale. I done handcuffed lightning, throwed thunder in jail. . . . Only last week, I murdered a rock, injured a stone, hospitalized a brick. I'm so mean, I make medicine sick.'"

"Wassled?" I say. "Who says that?"

"Muhammad Ali, that's who. And you, once your tongue starts behaving. Now, you'd better get going. Oh, take these too, to get started."

He hands me two books from his Ali collection. "We'll talk more about your project and work on this rhyme next week. Sound good?"

"*Thoundth th*well," I say, laughing as I grab my stuff.

Mr. Simms fakes an uppercut at my chin.

"You'd better run!" he yells after me as I hurry down the hall.

A couple of kids turn with curious looks. Instead of putting my head down, I look them in the eye and smile. I whistle "Back in Black" all the way to my next class.

Sleepovers

"**Q**uadruple grand champion!" yells Tyson, launching himself off the pullout couch in my basement and onto the floor cushions.

He just won our fourth straight match on Drag Race Double Dare.

"I call new game," I say, rolling over and sticking my hand in a bag of chips.

We're all set up for a perfect Friday night with our sleeping bags, snacks, and video games. Tyson's phone buzzes, and he scrambles to look at the text. His parents aren't hung up on "limiting children's access to technology" like mine are.

"It's Jenna. She wants to know if I'm at your house. Hang on—I'll FaceTime her," he says.

"No, wait," I say, but Tyson shoves the phone at me, and she's already answering.

"Oh, hi, Rory!" says Jenna. "What's up?"

I hear giggling in the background. "Nothing. Just hanging out with Ty. You?"

"Melanie's sleeping over tonight. We're working through her spelling flash cards. And we have a question for you."

"Salutations! Six days till the competition!" Melanie waves from behind Jenna's shoulder.

"Hi, Melanie!" says Tyson, practically knocking me over to get his face on the screen.

I push him away.

"What's the question?" I ask.

"Well, um, is your mom really going to take you to see Brent tomorrow morning?" asks Jenna. It had taken Brent longer to "settle in" than expected, so I'd had a reprieve from visiting him. But now my time was up.

"Yup."

"Do you think we could go with you?" Jenna asks.

"Don't you walk dogs at that adoption place then?" I ask.

"Yeah, but I could do it after."

Tyson is now jumping up and down behind the phone and pointing at himself. "Calm down," I say.

"What?" asks Jenna.

"No, not you. I was saying that to Tyson. Here. Talk to him while I go ask my mom."

I hand off the phone and Tyson presses it against his leg. "If your mom says they can go, can I come too?"

"What? Why would you want to?" I ask.

"Dude. It's Melanie Franklin. Pleeease?"

I shake my head. "I'll ask."

Tyson lifts the phone and flashes a sideways peace sign at the camera. "Hello, ladies, what's up?"

I find Mom and Dad in the living room.

"Hey. Need something?" asks Mom.

"Yeah. Jenna and Melanie and Tyson all want to know if they can come with us when we go to see Bwent."

"Oh. Uh, I'm not sure. I mean, I don't mind, but let me call Mrs. Milliken and see if she thinks it's a good idea. I'll let you know."

She pulls out her phone, and I go back to the basement.

"Here comes Rory." Tyson waves me over.

"Hi again, Rory," says Jenna. "What did she say?"

"She's calling Mrs. Milliken. We'll call you guys back."

"Okay, thanks."

"Bye!" says Melanie.

There's a lot more giggling as they squish their faces together on the screen, waving until the call cuts off.

Tyson falls back on the couch and puts his hand over his heart. I throw a controller at him, and we start up a new game.

A little while later, Mom comes downstairs. "Sorry, guys, Mrs. Milliken thinks four is too many. Tell the girls maybe next time. But she says you can come along, Tyson. Brent's therapists have been talking about having him practice with some small groups."

"Practice what?" Tyson asks.

"He's . . . Brent is having trouble interacting socially with people since his brain injury. It's one of the things he's working on at Salmon Brook—his rehab place."

Huh. I know some other kids who could use that kind of therapy too.

"Are you up for that?" Mom asks.

"Sure," says Tyson. "Why not?"

"Great," I say with fake enthusiasm.

"Hey!" Mom smiles. "You just said *great*! Perfectly!"

"Did I? *Great.* Guess I did!" I say, hitting the *r* again.

"My man," says Tyson.

Mom climbs over our sleeping bags to kiss us each on the head.

"Mom! Stop!" I cross my arms over my face.

"I can do what I want," says Mom. "And you know what? You're good kids."

"Thanks, Mrs. Mitchell," says Tyson.

I get all twisted inside. I wish I were as good as she thinks I am. She doesn't know about the hidden part of me that doesn't care about Brent or how long it takes him to get better. I wonder what her smiling eyes would look like if she knew how I really felt.

"Don't stay up too late." She goes back up the stairs and closes the door behind her.

"Dude. Let's call the girls back and practice our *social interactions,*" says Tyson, winking.

"Tyson, you have issues."

"I know. Why else do you think I'd be friends with you?"

He wiggles his shoulders and reaches for his phone.

The New Brent

We're quiet on the drive to Salmon Brook the next morning. The radio is on low, and I move my fingers in time to the music, playing invisible guitar strings. As the song ends, we go up a long driveway past a frost-covered lawn. Mom finds a parking spot near a sleek white building.

Then she turns around to face us. "Before we go in, let me tell you a few things Mrs. Milliken described, so you know what to expect."

"You told me no tubes," I say.

"No tubes, I promise. Brent's breathing well on his own now. He's also up out of bed, which is one of the reasons this move happened. But because of his injuries, he has to wear a helmet at all times. So you'll see that. And he might use a wheelchair. I'm not sure. Sometimes he does when he gets tired." She stops for a breath.

"He still gets overwhelmed easily, so we'll do whatever the staff asks if that happens. Okay? We won't stay long, but this visit is going to mean a lot to Brent and his parents. And it means a lot to *me* to have you both here," she finishes.

We nod and slide out of the car. The cold morning air stings my face as we hustle into the building. Sun streams in through two huge windows, making the front entrance warm and bright.

"Cute," Mom says, pointing to a tower of pumpkins on a hay bale, draped with a sign that says *Thankful*. It smells better than the hospital. Not great, but more like floor cleaner than pee.

Mrs. Milliken is there to greet us.

"Hello!" she says, hugging Mom. "I'm so glad you're all here. Come on, I'll take you down to the multipurpose room. Brent just finished physical therapy."

We walk down a quiet hallway into a busy open space that looks like a gym on one side and a living room on the other. Most of the people there are sitting in wheelchairs. Others are lying on mats or walking between two parallel bars with a person holding on to them. Along the side wall, patients are pulled up to tables, using their hands to pedal things that look like small bike wheels, or picking up beanbags and dropping them in buckets.

Mrs. Milliken leads us to a corner where Brent is sitting with a woman who's wearing a name tag that says *Teresa*.

"Brent, your friends are here," Mrs. Milliken announces.

Like last time, I almost don't recognize him. He has a soft helmet on over buzz-cut hair. His eyes are open oddly wide. Spit is collected at the corners of his mouth. He stares at us and squints like he's trying to focus. He stands up.

"I don't want to be here!" he says.

He comes charging at me. Teresa stands up and grabs his arm before he can knock me over.

"Brent," she says, her voice firm and calm. "Your friends came to visit you. We're going to say hi and talk for a while. Sit down."

Brent goes back to his seat and scowls. He reaches a finger inside one of the holes in his helmet and picks at his scalp. There is a flat bandage over the spot on his neck where the breathing tube used to be.

"Hi, boys," says the woman, motioning for us to take a seat. "I'm Teresa, Brent's speech-language pathologist. I'm so glad you're here. We love to practice conversations, and I think he's getting a little sick of me!" She nods at Mrs. Milliken, and the two moms move a few steps away.

"Teresa's nice," says Brent in a monotone, scratchy voice that's way too loud. "She's pretty. You're pretty, Teresa."

He grips the edges of his chair and rocks side to side, like a little kid waiting for a show to start.

I look over at Tyson and raise my eyebrows. He shakes his head a tiny bit. He's rolling a quarter across his knuckles. Flip, flip, flip.

"Okay, thank you, Brent," says Teresa. "But remember, you can speak with your indoor voice. We can hear you just fine."

"Okay, *shhhhhh*," Brent whispers, a finger to his lips.

I rub my hands together like I'm cold, even though I'm actually starting to sweat.

"Now, let's try saying hi to your friends again," says Teresa. "It's nice of them to come see you, don't you think?"

He looks at us.

"Can you tell me who's here today?" Teresa prompts him.

Brent points at me and says, "That's Rory. He goes to speech therapy too. Do you know him?"

"No, I don't, but it's very nice to meet you, Rory," Teresa says.

I nod at her. I'm annoyed that he said that, but at the same time, I can tell from the way he's acting that he's not exactly thinking clearly. I know I shouldn't care that this lady knows I'm in speech therapy. After all, apparently now Brent is too, and his problems seem a lot bigger than one little missing sound.

"And who else?" asks Teresa.

"Tyson," he says, pointing at him. "Why are you here?"

"Hey, uh, what's up, Brent?" says Tyson.

"I want to go home!" Brent almost yells.

"We'll talk about that later," says Teresa. "Let's focus on your visitors. Now would be a good time for you to ask them something like, How are you? or What have you been up to? Go ahead, Brent."

"Noooooo!" he says, his voice rising.

The sound of it makes him grab his own ears, and he stomps his feet on the floor.

"Why am I still here? I want to be home!" His voice gets angrier and higher with each word.

Teresa presses her hands onto his knees and has him count to ten with her. Then she reminds him to breathe.

Mrs. Milliken pats Brent's shoulder and leans over to whisper in his ear. "It's okay, sweetie. Calm down. You'll go home soon. I promise."

Brent stops moving his legs. A second later he starts bawling.

I stare at him. Big gulping sobs erupt from his scrunched-up face. Tyson bounces his legs. I give my mom a *get us out of here* look.

"Guys, why don't we go over here so Brent can have a little break," says Mom. She points toward another sitting area where a hockey game is on TV.

We squish together on a small couch and watch the players slam each other up against the walls of the rink.

I look back over to where Brent is. He wipes snot and tears on his shirt while his mom and Teresa fuss over him. I was like that after my grandpa's funeral. Brent sat in my room with me while I cried into my pillow until it was sopping wet. Then he went downstairs and snuck me a piece of cake. Seems impossible, but that cake really did make things better.

Mrs. Milliken sees me looking and waves us back over.

Tyson pushes me in front of him.

"It's okay," says Teresa, motioning for us to sit. "Sometimes things feel overwhelming. It happens to all of us. That's why it's so important to remember this strategy: take a break, count to ten, then get ready to try again." It sounds like something the Louisville Lip might say to a sparring partner.

Brent nods, his face splotchy. "I hurt my brain," he says. "I'm getting better."

"That's right!" says Teresa, smiling.

"Yes, you are," says Mrs. Milliken. She sniffs and straightens her shirt.

Brent stands up and flicks his hands like he's shaking off water. "Do you guys want to see my room?" He's way too loud again.

Teresa clasps his arm and puts a finger over her lips.

"Want to?" he whispers.

What I really want to do is *float on*—straight out the front door, that is. I could lie and say I'm feeling sick and need to wait in the car. That would be so much easier than staying here. But Brent is excited and laughing now just as hard as he was crying a few minutes ago. Why can't *easy* and *right* always be the same thing?

Teresa tells Brent to keep looking at me and Tyson, his conversational partners, until we answer him.

"Sure," says Tyson. Then he nudges me.

"Yup. Let's do it."

Brent claps his hands.

He leads us down a long hallway with doors on both sides. Brent walks slowly next to Teresa, followed by the moms, and then me and Tyson. Right after we cross another hall, Tyson grabs my arm and pulls me against the wall.

"Dude, what?" I ask.

He puts his finger over his lips and peeks around the corner, then points for me to do the same.

There's a woman with her back to us, squeezing a mop in a bucket next to a big rolling cart of cleaning supplies.

"What?" I say again.

He shushes me and answers in a whisper. "Dude. That's Danny Pulaski's mom."

Announcements

"Good morning, Kensington Middle School!" Principal Perkins's too-cheerful voice greets us over the announcements on Monday.

"Congratulations to the cross-country team for clocking fantastic times at their meet over the weekend. And please join me in wishing good L-U-C-K to all students competing in the spelling bee this Thursday."

I reach over and grab Melanie's arm, making her raise her hand. She turns bright red.

"And now, a special word from your class representatives."

There is a scuffle of sound as the microphone is passed.

"Hello, fellow students!" a girl's voice shouts. "The one-month countdown to our winter dance has begun! Get psyched to Jingle Jam the Friday before winter break! Tickets available at lunchtime starting December first. Be ready to jingle and mingle!"

Then another voice joins her in a shrill whoop that makes the speaker squeal. I cringe, and then the sound abruptly clicks off.

People turn to each other and start talking about the dance.

"Quiet, please," says Mrs. Nash. "I want to see you concentrating on your morning work."

Right. And I want a Gibson Les Paul guitar for Christmas. I don't think it's going to work out for either of us. We didn't have dances in elementary school. This is a first.

Kids keep whispering, and the buzz lifts to a roar until Mrs. Nash asks if we'd like more work since we seem to be finished.

I'm happy to *not* talk about the dance. For one thing, when I try to dance, I look like I'm being attacked by imaginary bees. And the thought of dancing with girls, which would require asking them to dance, sounds about as much fun as wrassling alligators.

At lunch Jenna, Asha, and Melanie join us as usual. Jenna's wearing a new sweatshirt that says *Stop Testing and Tasting Animals.* I take a deep breath of butterscotch-scented air.

"So, how'd it go? What happened?" asks Jenna, squeezing in next to me.

"What?" I ask.

"Your visit to Brent!" says Jenna.

"Yeah, what was that like?" asks Asha.

"Honestly it kinda freaked me out," says Tyson, squirting a packet of ketchup on his fries. "He was shouting and crying and stuff. And he has to wear this helmet all the time. He doesn't even look like Brent."

"Yeah, it got kind of intense. But the place wasn't as bad as the hospital," I say.

"And he calmed down when we went to his room," says Tyson. "But it was still all kinds of messed up."

"I'm just glad it's done. I hope my mom doesn't make me go again. He's got new fwends. Let them visit," I say.

"Yeah, what's up with that?" asks Jett. "You two used to hang out. Then all of a sudden, you didn't."

I shift and cough. "Can we talk about something else?"

"Dance decorations!" Jenna says, pulling out a sign-up sheet. "I'm in charge of recruiting sixth graders to help. You guys should do it with us."

"I don't know," says Jett.

"You get out of last period a few minutes early if you do," says Asha.

"Hmm. In that case, I pick science," I say.

"C'mon, Rory, we need you. You can help make the song list for the DJ. Plus we'll all get to hang out after school," says Jenna. "It'll be a good time."

"Isn't the dance, like, weeks away?" Jett asks.

"I know, but we don't want the decorations to be totally basic. Or the music. Please?" asks Asha.

Melanie turns to Jett and Tyson. "Pretty please?"

"Why not?" says Tyson. "Anything to get out of class."

"Fine," says Jett. "As long as you tell me what to do."

"Rory?" Jenna asks after she writes their names in her notebook.

"Okay. If these guys do it, I guess I will too." I may be anti-dance, but I'm not exactly anti-hanging-out-with-Jenna.

"Our first school dance!" says Jenna, clapping her hands. "This is gonna be so fun!"

Danny stops behind Jenna and claps his hands too. "So fun!" he says in a high-pitched voice.

Jenna rolls her eyes.

Danny leans over the table to see the sign-up sheet. "You guys actually care about the dance? That's sad." He rubs the stubble on the side of his head and laughs.

"Why? It'll be more fun than spending a Friday night somewhere like, oh, I don't know, *Salmon Brook*," says Tyson.

"What're you talking about?" Danny's eyes squint almost closed.

"We visited Brent there this weekend," says Tyson. "You should go see him too. He's a friend of yours, right? I bet your *mom* could drive you there."

Danny steps forward and Tyson stands up.

Then someone calls, "Yo, Pulaski! You comin'?"

Danny backs away, keeping his eyes on Tyson. He bumps into a kid walking behind him and hisses, "Watch it!"

Ali's Brain

When I get to the speech room for study hall after lunch, the door is locked. Through the little window, I see Mr. Simms reading a book and bobbing his head around. I pound on the door a few times until he finally hears me. He's wearing earbuds.

"Sorry! Lost track of time," he says, looking up at the clock.

"Whatcha listening to?" I ask.

"Guns N' Roses. You know them?"

"Some. They sing 'Welcome to the Jungle'?"

"Yup, among many other amazing songs. Have you listened to this album?" He points to the picture on his screen: *Appetite for Destruction.*

I shake my head.

"Well, we shall have to continue your education on the subject of quality music," he says. He writes down the band name and a few album titles on a sticky note and hands it to me. "Did you check out the Metallica album I told you about?"

"Yup. So awesome. I play it when I'm mad."

"Me too! Major mood lifter. Thrash metal is the best for that."
Mr. Simms slams some air drums.

"Exactly!"

I look at the book he just put down: *Educating the Brain-Injured Child.*

"Is that about Bwent?" I ask.

"Um, yes. I'm looking forward to helping him when he comes back. It's been a while since I worked with someone with a brain injury. Not since graduate school, actually."

"I saw him this weekend," I say. "At his new place."

"You did? How'd it go?"

"It was tough," I say.

"In what way?"

I think about how scary the visit was, really, and how Mom still doesn't understand how much I didn't want to be there. It's too hard to explain it all, and I might cry if I talk about it, so I just shrug.

Mr. Simms puts his elbows on the table and makes a little hammock for his chin with his hands. He looks right at me. He's good at waiting.

"He was really loud," I say.

"Hmm."

"And he kind of acted . . . wild. Like, he said odd things and then totally flipped out about wanting to go home."

"That sounds pretty upsetting," says Mr. Simms.

I nod. I knew he would get it. My stomach is knotted up like I'm back at the rehab place.

"Truthfully, Rory, that kind of behavior is really common with a brain injury. It's not pleasant to watch, but it is a normal part of the recovery process," Mr. Simms says.

"That's what Bwent's mom said."

"She's right. You know how little kids sometimes say and do the first thing that comes to their mind? They haven't learned to control their impulses, so everything comes tumbling out," he says. "People can be like that after a brain injury too. And then they have to relearn that skill. But the good news is, Brent's working on it, and he *is* getting better."

I'm relieved when he says Brent is getting better, but I'm also worried. The new Brent scares me and makes me sad, but the old Brent kind of did too. I'm not sure which one I hope he turns out to be. Right now I do feel sorry for him. But when he comes back to school, how's he going to treat me?

"Let me show you something." Mr. Simms pulls up a video of Muhammad Ali holding a torch. "This is the 1996 Summer Olympics in Atlanta, Georgia. Ali is about to start the games."

He lets a little of the video play. "See how his hands shake, and he shuffles when he walks? And when he spoke, it was really quiet and garbled. He had Parkinson's disease, which is different from Brent's injury, but it's also a neurological problem."

We watch the flames rise in the cauldron on the video.

"That was the final fight in a long list of hardships for the champ." He sighs and stops the video.

"What do you mean long list?" I ask. "The guy was a champion. He won all the time!"

"Not all the time. And he almost missed winning a gold medal in the 1960 Olympics because they were held in Rome, and he was afraid of flying. He actually carried his own parachute with him on the plane. Everyone's afraid of something, Rory."

"Wow," I say.

I should suggest that to my mom. She's a complete mess on airplanes. Any sudden sound or movement, and she grabs Dad's hand and says stuff like "What was that? Is that normal?"

Mr. Simms pushes another book from his Ali collection toward me. "Here. Read. Take notes. Learn."

Then he puts his earbuds in again and turns back to his own book. I pull out a sheet of paper, but instead of taking notes, I draw a music staff and start composing my own version of the Olympic theme song. It's impossible to know what was going on in Ali's brain on that flight to Rome, but I try to match what I imagine he felt to the music in my head.

I start with the basic melody and add in sharps and flats to change the song from major to minor so it sounds eerie. Then I write a bunch of really low bass chords to show what Ali was probably thinking: I hope this plane doesn't crash.

Too soon the bell rings, ending fourth period. I tap on Mr. Simms's shoulder and wave goodbye.

Near the gym, Danny is holding some kid's hat out of reach. I think about what it would feel like to walk around knowing your mom has to clean floors instead of being a manager at a big company because she stole money. I'll bet that soundtrack is even darker and heavier than thrash metal. But it doesn't make me hate him any less.

Ali and Me

I scowl in front of my bedroom mirror. My speech cards are in a pile on my desk, and I grab the top one and read, "'My face is so pwitty, you don't see a scaw, which pwoves I'm the king of the *rr*ing by faw.'" I jut out my chin and put my left fist up under it.

I eye the stack of books next to my bed that I've collected for the biography project. I didn't work on it at all last weekend—there was no way I was going to follow up the visit with Brent by doing schoolwork—and now I'm procrastinating some more by practicing my *r*'s.

I get right up close to the mirror and look inside my mouth.

"Pewwwrrr." I watch my lazy tongue struggle to get and stay in the right position.

"Aaahhhhhrrrrrrr." That one's a little easier.

"Pewwwrrrrrr, ahhhhhrrrrr," I repeat. I wonder how Muhammad Ali would have felt about his words being part of my speech therapy.

"What in the heck are you doing in here?" asks Dad, peeking his head around the door.

I wipe my mouth with the back of my hand. "Nothing."

"Didn't sound like nothing. Whatcha working on?"

My fingers fold the index card into a little paper taco. I try to think of some excuse that will explain why I'm staring into the mirror squawking like a deranged pirate. But I don't want to dig a hole I can't get out of, and there's pretty much nothing that can explain this but the truth.

"My ahhhhrrrr sounds," I say.

"Hey, listen to you!" says Dad. He motions toward the card. "Is that your speech homework?"

"Yeah." I show him the quote and point to the stack of others. "Muhammad Ali."

"Oh, yeah, you told me about that. Can I hear it?"

"What?" I don't want to do this in front of someone else.

"Come on." He pushes over a pile of dirty clothes so he can sit on my bed. "Let me hear you."

"Um . . ."

In the mirror, I can see that I'm turning red. *Relax*, Mr. Simms would say. *Float like a butterfly.* I turn toward Dad. I rock from one foot to the other and then repeat the rhyme, stopping to get my tongue in position and emphasizing the *r*'s the best I can.

Dad grins and grabs one of the other cards. He dances around me and jabs with his free hand. He reads it out, hitting all the rhymes—and the *r*'s—exactly right. "'I done wrassled with an alligator, I done tussled with a whale. I done handcuffed lightning, throwed thunder in jail. . . . Only last week, I murdered a rock, injured a stone, hospitalized a brick. I'm so mean, I make medicine sick.'"

We circle and fake-punch each other.

"You think that's fast?" I say in my best Ali voice, ducking under his swinging arm. "Too slow to go with the flow, old man."

"But I'm the greatest!" says Dad. "Look out little man! I'm gonna crush you!"

"Come at me!" I say.

He grabs my waist, wrestles me to the bed, and tickles my sides.

"What am I?" he asks. "What am I?"

"Okay, okay. The greatest! Stop!" I'm gasping for breath.

"Hey!" he says, letting me up. "That sounded good! I mean the *way* you said it. You said greatest."

"I did? Grrreatest. Well, then *I'm* the greatest!"

"You *are* a great kid, Rory," Dad says, pressing down my hair where it flipped up.

"You have to say that, Dad. I'm all you've got!"

"No, really." His lips pull into a straight line. "Mom told me about your visit to Brent's rehab place. She said it seemed like you'd rather have stayed on the sidelines."

"Well . . . yes."

"You know, it can be hard when one of your favorite players gets traded to another team. You're used to rooting for them, and then suddenly you don't want to anymore."

I nod. This might be one of his better sports analogies.

"I think maybe you two were starting to work out of different playbooks even before he got hurt. Am I right?"

I should tell him. I know I should. But I don't want to ruin the fun we just had.

"Kind of," I say. "He's basically hanging out with a new group of guys now. And I'm not in it."

I grab the coil of pipe cleaner from my nightstand and tap my finger against the sharp tip.

"Well, you were a good sport to go along with the visit. This brain injury business is tough. And you know how your mom loves helping people."

"Tell me about it."

We both laugh, and I notice we have the same kind of gravelly chuckle. Dad's is lower, like the bass line. And mine's the melody. But the harmony is awesome. I pick up one of the Ali books and look at his picture on the cover.

"Mistuh Simms told me Ali had something going on too." I point to my head. "P-something?"

"Yeah. Parkinson's disease. Some people say all those beatings he took in the ring didn't help, you know? Too many hits to the head. But thankfully he had a lot of good years after his boxing career. I remember seeing on TV how he helped free some hostages in Iraq once. He even won some kind of peace award, I think." He points to the book. "I'll bet it's all in there. You're supposed to be doing research for that big project, right?"

"I was just getting to that."

Dad pushes on my shoulder and stands up. "Okay. Back to work, then."

I hear him whistling all the way down the stairs. I look in the mirror again. My face is still red, but this time it's not from embarrassment.

"I'm the grrreatest of all time," I whisper. "The greatest!"

No Hitting

Jett, Tyson, and I loop our bikes in lazy circles on my driveway. "Let's go over to the dirt-bike path," says Jett, wiping his glasses with the edge of his Red Sox jersey.

"Nah," I say.

I unzip the fleece jacket Mom bugged me to put on. Today—the Saturday after Thanksgiving—is weirdly warm.

"C'mon, why not? We haven't been there in forever," says Tyson.

I don't feel like riding past where Brent got hit to hang out in the place that reminds me of why we aren't friends anymore.

"Just don't feel like it," I say.

"But there's nothing else to do!" says Jett. "I'm so bored!"

"Plus it means we ride past Melanie's house!" says Tyson. "Race ya!"

They take off. After a second I follow. The warm sun bakes into my shoulders and the muscles in my legs burn as I pedal up the huge hill on Maplewood Street. My tires crunch through piles of dried brown leaves bunched around the storm drains.

Then I sit back and enjoy the sweet reward of coasting all the way down the other side.

I catch up to the guys at the bottom of the hill, and we turn toward Melanie's. The way we're riding takes us right past Brent's house. I concentrate on the pavement in front of me and pedal faster, but as I pass his mailbox, I hear a small voice call out, "Hi, Rory!"

I tap my brakes. Maggie's sitting on her front steps holding some chalk.

"You guys go ahead—I'll catch up," I call as I make a U-turn.

"Hi," I say to Maggie, coasting my bike up the driveway.

"Hi," she says again.

"Whatcha doin'?" I ask.

"Drawing cranberry sauce." She traces pink swirls on the cement next to her.

"Oh, I see that now."

"I spilled it during our Turkey Day dinner."

"Oops!"

"Yeah, and it got on Brent, and he tried to hit me, and my dad had to grab his arms and lay him down on the floor."

Whoa. "Bwent's home?" I ask.

"He was, but he's back at his get-better place now."

She draws a purple circle around the pink blob.

"You talk like a kindergartner," she says, looking back up at me.

Coming from anyone else, this would sting. I'd probably get mad and ride away. But I know she's just being honest, the way little kids are.

"I'm glad Bwent got to visit at Thanksgiving," I say, and I mean it.

"But hitting's not nice," she says.

"No. It's not. I guess he isn't all the way fixed yet."

"I hope he hurries."

"He will." I hear the guys calling to me. "Gotta go. See you, Maggie."

"Bye," she says.

As I ride away, I look back over my shoulder and see her clutching the chalk, staring at her messy picture.

"There you are!" says Jett as I glide around the corner.

"Melanie's not home," says Tyson. "Let's keep going."

I follow them on autopilot along the familiar paved bike path. Then we turn and cut through the thick pine trees to a cleared area where kids have built a few dirt hills. I was worried it would be crowded, but no one else is here. We each take a spin on the circuit, trying to jump the highest.

"Dude, you used to be here with Brent every time I came," says Tyson.

He jerks back on his handlebars, trying to pop a wheelie.

I rest my bike against some shrubs and sit down, digging at the hard ground with a nearby stick.

Jett drops his bike and throws pinecones against a big stump. "Yeah. How come you stopped doing stuff with him?"

"I've been wanting to ask you that too," admits Tyson. "What happened?"

The memory flashes bright and unwelcome in my mind. The dirt was wet that day, almost muddy. I heard voices as I rode up the path, and I found Brent here with a bunch of guys. He'd been away at a wrestling match, and I was happy to see he was back.

I shake my head to clear the image. I can't tell even my best friends the real reason Brent and I don't hang out anymore.

"Nothing happened," I say. "He totally got into the whole 'team WWE' thing and kind of ditched me—that's all. His loss, ya know?"

"I always wondered why you hung out with him so much in the first place," says Jett. "He was never all that friendly to me."

"Same," says Tyson, riding back and forth in front of us.

Back when Brent and I were friends, I never noticed or thought about that. I was always either with these guys or with Brent—never both, though I hadn't kept them separate on purpose.

"Dudes," I say. "You didn't miss anything."

After a while we each take off toward our own house. I pedal slowly, thinking about Brent and steering my handlebars back and forth so I'm riding in an S shape. My thoughts change direction almost every time my front wheel does. One minute I feel sorry for him and hope he gets better. The next I think how lucky Tyson and Jett are that they never got close to him.

I pump my legs and pick up speed until I'm riding as fast as I can. Away from bad memories. Away from sad sisters. Away from my stupid *r* sounds. The only problem is, I can't pedal fast enough to get away from my own self.

Tickets and Snowflakes

Halfway through third-period math, it starts snowing. In a few months, it won't be any big deal. But the first snow of the season amps everyone up. On the way to lunch, kids shout and push to get a good spot at the courtyard windows, watching to see if it's sticking.

An eighth grader with gel-spiked hair and red cheeks clomps through the hallway in untied boots, yelling, "Snow day!"

Jett and I turn the corner and hit a student-council blockade right in front of the cafeteria. There's a table set up, and kids are selling tickets to the dance. Nearby a girl shakes her pom-poms high and low.

"Two more weeks till the winter dance! Grab your tickets while you have a chance! Woo!" she yells.

I duck to avoid a high kick to the face.

The money Mom gave me this morning for my ticket is curled in my sweaty hand. Tyson is already in line. He waves us over.

"I don't know. I don't think I'm gonna go," I say.

"C'mon. Fall in, cadet," says Jett, pulling me next to him. "We're already signed up to help with the decorations anyway."

"You mean dorkorations?" says Danny, pushing in next to us. "Of course you're signed up for that, Rory. Gotta make sure there are changing tables in the baby area, right?"

Someone giggles. A rush of heat passes through me.

"What's the holdup here?" asks a lunch monitor, noticing the crowd at her door. "Let's move this table off to the side."

Danny slinks away as she's talking. When we get to the front of the line, Tyson asks for three tickets before I can stop him.

Inside the cafeteria Jenna is already at our usual spot, dipping carrots into hummus.

"Where were you guys?" she asks.

"Getting our golden tickets," says Tyson, holding his up.

"Nice! And are you guys going to stay after today—for decorations?"

"I don't know," I say.

Jenna frowns and chews on her lip. She takes out a pencil, writes something on her napkin, and slides it to me. I look at it under the table.

It says *I hope you do.*

The words make me feel like I'm floating up out of my seat. I pinch the note between my fingers, like I'm a balloon and it's the string.

"Hey! You came! Over here!" Asha waves us to a table where a couple of girls are squeezing glitter glue along the edges of large snowflakes cut out of thick paper.

Across the gym others are hole-punching white copy paper, making "snow." Some guys are sword fighting with empty wrapping-paper rolls. Mr. Leigh, the PE teacher, is gulping coffee and shouting at kids to stay off the gymnastics mats.

"We did come," says Tyson. "How may we be of assistance?"

"Ooh! Can one of you quiz me while I paint?" asks Melanie, looking up from a nearby table where she's working on a large canvas welcome banner.

"I'll do it! Me!" says Tyson. Then he bows and says, "That is, it would be my honor, Ms. Champion."

I roll my eyes.

"Yeah, you already won, right?" asks Jett. "More studying?"

"If you win at the middle-school level, you get to go to districts!" says Melanie, her eyes bright. She holds up a huge book and hands it to Tyson. "I'm trying to learn all these. It's kinda fun."

"You have an odd but admirable sense of fun," says Jett.

"So what should Jett and I do?" I ask Jenna.

"Here," says Jenna, handing us a stack of paper. "This is the DJ's song list. Can you guys mark the ones he should play?"

It's a great collection. Not all the music is my style, but I know what most kids are into. In my mind, I can hear which songs should go first, when to slow it down, and how to rev people back up.

But Jett is bored. He rolls a tube of glitter back and forth. "You know what we need? A little R and R. I wish it were winter break already."

"I heard that Brent might come back to school after the break," says Asha.

"That's pretty hard to believe," says Jett. "I mean, based on what these guys said after they visited him."

"Yeah," says Tyson. "He's all kinds of messed up. Better have a padded room ready!"

Jett and I laugh.

"You guys are being jerks," says Jenna. She walks over to the other side of the gym.

"Touchy," says Tyson, stopping to watch her go. "It was just a joke."

"Hang on," I say. I get up and join Jenna at the hole-punchers.

"Hey." I tap her arm. "That wasn't nice of us. I know you like Bwent. And we shouldn't laugh at him."

"What?" Jenna tilts her head up to look at me. "I don't like Brent! Well, not in that way. I just think it's not right to make jokes about someone who's hurt."

"You don't *like* him, like him?" I ask.

"No. You thought I did?"

"Well, yeah. What about the note you gave him? And wanting to visit?"

She leans in and whispers, "Duh. That note was from Melanie. She's the one who likes him."

I look over to where Melanie and Tyson are hanging up the big Jingle Jam sign. He's wobbling the ladder on purpose so she has to hold it tighter, and they're laughing. This is going to kill him.

"Oh, wow. I had no idea." My heart does this weird seesaw thing where it goes down for Tyson but up for me. Brent is *Melanie's* crush! *Don't smile. Stop it, lips!*

"Yeah, no offense, but sometimes guys are not too bright in this department," she says.

"Hey, cut us some slack. We try."

"Whoa! Rory! Cool." Jenna is smiling at me.

"What?" I ask.

"Sorry, I'm so used to you sounding a certain way. And you just said *try*."

"Did I?"

I'm embarrassed that she noticed my speech. But at least it was for a good reason, not a bad one.

"Yeah, I guess I did. I've been wuhking, um, working on it. I still go to speech." Geez. Why did I say that? Stop talking. Stop talking.

"My brother does too," she says. "He sounds a lot like you, actually."

"What are you two being so serious about?" asks Jett, coming over to hand me the music list. "Slow dancing?" He holds his arms up and sways.

"Dude, shut up!" I flash a sideways glimpse at Jenna.

"Yeah, whatever, we're just friends!" says Jenna.

Just friends. The words hit me square on the chin with the force of one of Ali's right-handed swings. I see myself falling in slow motion, headed for the mat.

"Okay, students," calls Mr. Leigh. "Step up the pace! Only two more decoration meetings until Mr. Perkins makes me surrender my gym to you completely. Can we get some help here putting this paper snow into garbage bags?"

Jenna walks over to where he's pointing, and her steps do the counting: one, two, three, four, five, six, seven, eight, nine, ten. Knockout.

Courage and Strength

"**H**ey, it's the Rorinator!" says Mr. Simms when I walk into the speech room the next week. He takes a handful of candy canes from a cellophane-wrapped box and puts them into his pencil holder.

"Hey, Mistuh Simms," I say.

"Who?" He looks behind him.

"Huh?" I'm confused.

"I don't know any *Mistuh* Simms."

Oh. Tongue tip back. Sides against teeth. "Mister*rr* Simms," I say. "Happy?"

"Very! Very happy, Rory. You are doing so amazingly well. Let's see what else you've got for me."

I spread my index cards out on the table.

"Let's do this one," he says, pointing.

I read it. "'My face is so pwitty, you don't see a scaw, which means I'm the king of the ring by faw.'"

"Nice job on the initial *r* in *ring*," he says. Then he circles *scar* and *far*. "Those are pirate words. *Arrrgh*. Try it."

"*Arrgh.* Sc . . . *arrgh.* Sc*arrr. Arrgh.* Fa*rrr.*"

"Yes, yes, yes!" He gets out a piece of paper and writes the word *pretty.*

"Okay. See this?" He circles the *pr.* "This is really two sounds, *p* and *er.* Try them separately first."

"Puh . . . errr. Pewwrrruh. Pewwlllrruh. Pwitty. Ugh, I can't do it! I sound awful." I tilt my head back and blow a raspberry at the ceiling.

"Okay, let's skip that for now. But listen to how well you're doing on the other ones! Your *r* is way better than it was, can you hear that?" Mr. Simms asks.

I have to admit it's true. "Sometimes I even say something wight, *right,* without thinking about it."

"That. Is. So. Cool!" says Mr. Simms. He gets really excited about speech stuff.

"I hate how long it's taking me, though," I say.

"I hear ya. I'm no good at being patient, either. Imagine how painful it must have been for Muhammad Ali when he was waiting to be allowed to box again," Mr. Simms says.

Everything makes him think of Muhammad Ali. "What do you mean?"

"Ah, I see you're really throwing yourself into your biography project research," he teases.

"Um." I search for an excuse. "Why don't you tell me about it, and I'll take notes?"

"You're sneaky. But okay," he says.

I pull out a notebook, and Mr. Simms shows me some pictures from one of his big glossy books.

"You've heard of the Vietnam War, right?" he says.

"Yeah."

"At the time, the government was drafting guys over the age of eighteen to fight in Vietnam. Eventually Ali's name was picked."

He shows me a picture in the book, and I copy down what it says underneath it: *1966, Local Draft Board No. 47.*

"But here's the thing. Remember I told you about him converting to a new religion? There's a specific branch of Islam in the United States called the Nation of Islam. Ali was really dedicated to the leaders and what they taught, including that fighting in any war was wrong. So when the draft board called his name, he flat-out refused to step forward, which was against the law. It was a very gutsy move."

"A guy who fought all the time didn't want to fight?" I ask, taking a break from writing.

"Right. But there's a big difference between knocking someone out with your fists in a controlled sport and killing someone with a gun on a battlefield, wouldn't you say?"

I nod. "So what happened to him?"

"He was arrested and sentenced to five years in jail."

"He went to jail?" I can't believe it.

"Actually his lawyers appealed his case right away, and he was free during that time. But not exactly free to do what he wanted. The boxing world was really angry. They took away his heavyweight title, which he had just won from Sonny Liston. And he wasn't allowed to book any professional fights."

"What? He must have hated that!"

"Yeah. But no matter what happened, he never backed down from his decision. Even when he faced hard consequences, he held on to the belief that what he was doing was right. It's funny, but by taking a stand against the government and *not fighting*, that was how he became a real symbol of courage and strength."

I scribble more quick notes, trying to write this all down.

"Okay, enough history," says Mr. Simms, breaking my concentration. "We only have ten more minutes. Let's do more *r* work."

"Okay." I sigh.

"Darts?" he asks.

"Dawts!"

He lifts one eyebrow. "Excuse me?"

I take a deep breath. My tongue sloshes around as I try to make it go from the front where it's making the *d* sound to the back and sides for *r*.

"Daahrrrts," I finally manage.

Mr. Simms grins and hands me a dart. "You say the sound right, you get to throw one. If you don't, I get to. One point every time the magnet sticks. And whoever gets the most points wins."

I hurl the first one at the ripped-up *R* still taped to the board on the back of his door. It lands in the green zone. "Yes!"

He keeps calling out words for me. *War. Draft. Arrested. Religion.*

It's hard. I don't get all of them. But when the bell rings, I'm winning ten to four.

Winter Dance

I bolt from the car as soon as Mom stops at the curb in the drop-off circle.

"Pick you up at nine!" she calls out the window.

I give her a quick wave and jog to catch up to Tyson and Jett, who are standing in the short line of kids outside the gym. Thumping music swells through the open doors. When we walk in, it's kind of exciting to see how different the space looks. It's mostly dark, and the huge glittery snowflakes hanging from the ceiling sparkle whenever they catch a bit of light. Tyson goes straight for the food, and then we grab a spot against the wall.

"Whoa! Jenna Kim in a skirt. That's not something you see every day," says Tyson, pointing across the room.

He sticks his tongue straight into his cone of popcorn and retrieves a few pieces. Jenna's skirt has little flecks of silver on it like the snowflakes.

"Alllll right, Kensington!!" says a booming voice. "Are you ready to shake things up?" The DJ walks out onto the middle of the floor. "Don't be shy, don't be shy! Let's make some Kensington commotion!"

A bunch of kids move toward him, clearing little paths in the thin layer of hole-punched snow.

"Coming?" asks Tyson. He spins once and spills some popcorn on the floor.

"Nah, I'm good," I say.

"Yeah, me too. I need to do some reconnaissance first," says Jett.

"I'll give you one song to loosen up, boys. You know my motto: Never let 'em see you drop. Don't sink to the bottom . . ." He stops and points at us.

"Gotta float to the top," we mumble in unison.

"C'mon, say it like you mean it! Float to the top!" Tyson dances off.

We watch him join a group in the middle of the floor. He keeps going the wrong way and bumping into kids. But he's laughing, and it looks like he's having a great time. I move my head a little in rhythm with the music and shift from foot to foot. My body wants to go out there and be goofy like Tyson, but my mind makes me stay right where I am.

The next song starts before the first one even ends—the beat of "Good Feeling" playing right into the tempo of "Kick It." The DJ is following my song recommendations! More kids go out on the floor and start jumping and moving.

The music is so loud it makes it hard to talk, which makes it easier for me to relax and blend in. I look around the room. The huge empty boxes we wrapped with shiny paper and bows are stacked in pyramids. I notice that the messy ones Tyson and I did are hidden in the back by the food tables. A lot of other kids are standing against the wall like Jett and me. Danny is near the door with a bunch of guys. He starts imitating the DJ's moves, and the group laughs. They move like a giant amoeba across the room toward the food.

I check the time. It's only seven o'clock.

"Wanna get something to eat?" asks Jett.

"Nah, you go ahead, though."

He walks over to the table and starts talking to one of his baseball friends. I undo the second button on the collared shirt Mom made me wear and check the clock again. Seven-oh-one. Then a Bon Jovi song I marked on the list, "It's My Life," comes on. Last month it rose from the dead in the soundtrack of a new zombie movie. I could definitely dance to this.

I decide to go for it. I'm headed toward Tyson when suddenly the room gets quieter. The music is still playing, but it's like all the conversations stop. Something's going on at the entrance to the gym. I move around so I can get a good look.

No. Way.

Surprise

B rent is standing in the doorway. Behind him are his mom and an assistant teacher from the resource room, the one who sometimes does lunch duty and lets us call him by his first name, Angelo. Someone starts to clap. Other people join in, and then everyone's applauding.

Kids rush over, and Angelo steps in front of Brent and holds his pointer finger straight up, to tell them to say hi one at a time. A loose line forms, like Brent's a rock star giving out autographs. He's not wearing the helmet. His hair is still shaved short, and a long dark scar snakes across the side of his head. He has a huge grin on his face.

Brent's arrival makes me miss the Bon Jovi song. And now the room quiets down again because "Amazed" starts to play—the first slow dance. I quickly join Jett by the food, grab a piece of pizza, and take a huge bite. I don't want to even think about asking someone to dance.

A few couples move to the middle of the room and stand there, hands on hips and shoulders, rocking side to side. I look up to see where Tyson went. He's standing under the arch of aluminum-foil icicles, getting a group photo with Jenna and Melanie and Asha. Apparently he hasn't gotten up the nerve to ask anyone to slow dance either. And from the way he's smiling and laughing, he definitely hasn't noticed how much Melanie keeps looking at Brent. I watch Jenna make different poses for the camera, and my bite of pizza does a little flip on its way to my stomach.

Mrs. Milliken and Angelo lead Brent to a section of the bleachers near us. I turn slightly and avoid eye contact, especially when Danny walks over. But Jett nudges me to look when Brent responds to Danny's high-five by jumping up and grabbing him in a tight hug.

"Hey, chill," says Danny, turning his head and trying to get free.

Angelo stands up and pulls Brent's hands away. The other kids back up.

The next song kicks in with a fast hip-hop beat, and most of the kids who were crowded around Brent rush back to the dance floor.

"Work!" someone shouts, and a large group of girls starts doing the exact same moves, like they learned them in a dance class or something.

Tyson comes over with Jenna, Melanie, and Asha and points to the soda Jett is holding.

"Sure. Finish it," says Jett.

"Thanks." Tyson guzzles the rest in one big gulp. He lets out an epic burp, which makes Jett and me crack up.

"Nice," says Asha, bumping her shoulder into him.

"Gross," says Melanie.

There are only a few kids gathered around Brent now.

"Should we go say hi?" asks Jenna, nodding toward Brent.

"Let's!" Melanie pulls on her braids and wraps them under her chin.

"I'll go too," says Asha, linking arms with Jenna on one side and Melanie on the other. She looks back at us. "You guys coming?"

"Not right now," says Jett.

I nod in agreement. Hard pass.

"Maybe later," says Tyson.

As the girls approach Brent, the song starts to fade, and a super-quick techno beat comes in.

The DJ says, "I have one question for you, Kensington!"

He cranks the volume and blasts "Turn Down for What."

Brent stands up and shouts, "I love this song! I'm going to dance!"

Angelo stays right with Brent as he makes his way to the dance floor, lifting each foot up high and setting it down solidly before taking the next step. He looks like he's walking through thick mud. When he reaches the center area, he starts bobbing his whole body up and down with his arms stretched out for balance. He's looking down at his own legs.

"He reminds me of my little cousin," says Jett.

"Ouch," says Tyson.

It's hard not to stare.

Brent lifts his head and sees Danny and the clump of guys with him, watching from the sidelines. He waves to them and throws himself off balance. Angelo grabs Brent's arm to steady him, but Brent pushes his hand away.

Suddenly the synthesized throbbing cuts to abrupt silence.

"One second, folks. Technical difficulties," the DJ says into the microphone.

The room seems bigger and darker without the sound from the speakers filling it up.

In the middle of all that quiet, Brent shouts, "Get away from me! I don't need help!"

Everyone turns to look.

Brent waves his arms at Angelo, who grabs them and twists, wrapping Brent in a tight hug from behind.

Kids near them back off in a widening circle, whispering. A few teachers come closer, trying to help.

"Leave me alone!" Brent whines, straining against Angelo's hold.

Mrs. Milliken gets right in front of Brent, her eyes almost as wild as his.

"Please calm down, honey," she begs. "The deal was we were only going to stay for a little bit, remember? We'll leave now."

She nods at Angelo, and the two of them move Brent across the floor and out the side doors. We can hear him yelling from the parking lot until the outer doors clang shut.

For a moment everyone in the room stands as frozen as the winter decorations around us. It was one thing to see Brent fall apart at the treatment place, but it feels more serious—bigger—to see it play out right here in the middle of the school gym.

"Okkaaaay, Kensingtonnnn!" the DJ's voice booms, cracking the icy silence.

A quiet, smooth song starts to play.

"Sorry for the delay. Now, everyone grab your favorite person, because it's time to sloooow things down a bit."

Kids start moving and talking again.

"Whoa," says Jett.

"That was intense," says Tyson.

But I decide to be like the DJ and act like nothing happened. Like all that matters is getting to the next song. If Brent and I were still friends, I'd be stuck thinking about what I just saw and feeling bad about it. Good thing we're not. It makes it easier to focus on what I'm going to do next.

Before, I wasn't sure I even wanted to be here. But at least I *can* be here. I mean, I'm not a great dancer, and I've got a wonky *r*, but right now I'm going to focus on things I can control.

"Boys," I say, standing up, "it's time to ask someone to dance."

Slow Dancing

"**Y**ou serious? I'm in!" Tyson jumps to his feet and nods at the girls, who are coming back to where we're sitting.

"Did you guys see that?" asks Jenna.

"Unfortunately I'm pretty sure everyone's radar picked it up," says Jett.

"Yeah, but you want to know what I see now?" asks Tyson. "A completely open dance floor. Whaddya say, Melanie?"

"Sorry, I really don't feel like dancing." She's watching the door that Brent went out.

"Sure, no biggie." Tyson's shoulders sag a little as he follows her gaze. "You're missing out on my signature moves, though."

I clear my throat. *Here I go. Gonna ask Jenna Kim to dance. I can do this. Hang on, how long has this song been playing? Is it about to end? Maybe I should wait till the next one.*

There's a tug on my arm.

"C'mon, Rory. We're dancing." Asha grabs my hand and pulls me out to the floor before I can think of how to answer.

"Hold up, I wanna come too," calls Tyson. "Jenna? Help me out?"

"Sure," she says.

Jenna's eyes flit to me as Tyson leads her to the dance floor, and we share a quick smile. Maybe the next song.

The four of us push in among the other couples. Asha and I stand facing each other for a second, and I'm not sure what to do next. She puts a hand on each of my shoulders. I put my hands as lightly as possible on her waist because that's what I see the other guys doing. We start to make super-slow circles, around and around. I concentrate on my feet, making sure not to step on hers.

"That was pretty weird what just happened with Brent, huh?" she asks.

"Yeah."

"I know Melanie is bummed she didn't get to dance with him," she says.

"I think Jenna might feel the same," I say.

"Huh?" Asha leans back, her head tilted to the side.

"She told me she doesn't like him that way, but then she's always asking how he's doing, so I don't know if I believe her." I shrug.

"What? No. Duh, Rory. It's not Brent she likes." Asha rolls her eyes at me.

"So there is someone?" I spin so I can see Jenna over Asha's shoulder. "Who is it?"

"She won't tell me, but I think I know," Asha replies.

"Who?" My voice squeaks. Be calm. Be cool.

Asha pulls on my shoulders and moves us right next to Jenna and Tyson.

"Switch!" she says, spinning away from me and pushing in between them.

Tyson grabs Asha's hands and they start doing some sort of tango-like dance back and forth.

Jenna and I hold on with feather fingers and sway side to side, watching them and laughing. I'm glad we have something to look at because I'm too nervous to say anything.

As the song winds down, the DJ tells us to enjoy our holiday break and announces the last dance. The music has a pulsing beat and the words tell us to jump, jump! The girls pull Jett onto the floor with us.

Tyson changes the words to the song and shouts to the beat, "Don't sink to the bottom!"

This time Jett and I yell back, "Float! Float!"

We all bounce around and knock into each other. I have no idea what I'm doing, but for once I don't care. Loud music, no talking. I wish the song would never end.

All Good Things

Sunshine blasts through the gap in my bedroom curtains. I squeeze my eyes tight and burrow into my rumpled sheets, listening to the quiet movements of my parents and drinking in the smell of syrup and bacon. It's the last morning of winter break. I flip onto my stomach and grab the edges of my bed. Two weeks of absolute freedom are almost over. I'll miss sleeping in and playing guitar whenever I feel like it—which was sometimes all day.

I finally get my eyes to stay open so I can look at my favorite Christmas present. On Christmas Eve, as we were getting ready to go over to Mr. Garland's for "holiday cheer," I heard a knock at our door and was surprised to find Jenna standing there under the porch light. I stepped outside and closed the door behind me. It had just started to snow.

I said something genius like, "Hey, what's up?"

She handed me what looked like a glob of wrapping paper that had gotten into a fight with some tape.

"This is for you," she said.

Just then Mom opened the door. "Jenna! Hello! Rory, what on earth? Aren't you going to invite Jenna inside? It's freezing out here."

"That's okay, Mrs. Mitchell. I gotta go! Merry Christmas!" She ran off.

We went straight to Mr. Garland's party after that. The whole night I couldn't wait to get home and open her present, which I had shoved into my coat pocket. But Mr. Garland had talked me into playing Christmas carols on his wife's old piano, and people kept giving me requests.

When I was finally alone in my room, I tore off the wrapping and found a brass capital *R*, about the size of my palm. It's heavy, like a paperweight. I put it on my dresser and stared at it, feeling bad that I hadn't gotten Jenna anything. Was I supposed to?

Now, staring at it again, I watch how the gold color reflects the sun that streams in through my window. I reach over to my nightstand drawer and take out what I've been working on for Jenna. It's a little eight-note melody with a letter above each note: T-H-A-N-K Y-O-U. But the rest I'm having trouble with.

So far, I have *Dear Jenna, Thanks for the R. I'm sorry I didn't get you anything.*

I can't figure out how to sign it. *Love? Your Friend? Sincerely?* Finally I write *Thanks again, Rory.*

I hear my dad's footsteps on the stairs, so I scramble to hide the paper back in my drawer. When he opens the door, I'm sitting up in bed with the blankets perfectly folded at my waist.

"Hey there. I was wondering if you were up yet. Tyson's here," he says.

I jump out of bed and pull a sweatshirt over my pajama top. When I get downstairs, Tyson is at the kitchen counter, spinning around on a stool and having what I'm guessing is a second breakfast. His mom would never let him leave home without eating first, and my mom would never let him refuse food here.

"There you are, sleepyhead," says Mom as I slide in next to Tyson.

"Hope you saved me some," I say, pointing to his waffles.

"Don't worry." Mom pulls two more from the freezer and pops them in the toaster for me.

"You ready for school to start tomorrow, Ty?" she asks.

"Nope!" He reaches for another strip of bacon.

"Ditto," I say.

"Well, all good things must come to an end," says Mom. "I wonder how they're feeling over at the Millikens'. Brent's been cleared to start back with you guys. I hope he's ready for this big step . . ." Her voice fades to a whisper as she says the last part. She's looking out the window, not at us.

Tyson raises his eyebrows at me. After the dance, Brent's meltdown was all anyone could talk about. But then winter break started, and I honestly haven't thought about him since. I really don't want to think about him now either.

It was so great to have a break from everything. No worrying about my speech. No dodging Danny and his constant stupid *baby* comments. No reminders of Brent and his brain injury or what went down between us that horrible day last spring, and how I should forget about that and feel bad about his injury. But tomorrow Brent's going to be everywhere—classes, our lockers, lunch. He's even going to invade the speech room.

Mr. Simms had told me before break. "Just so you know, Brent will be here Mondays, Wednesdays, and Fridays after lunch next semester."

But those are the days I hang out with Mr. Simms in the speech room for study hall.

"Why? His speech is fine."

"Speaking clearly is one thing, but language skills are another. A lot of my job is about helping kids comprehend and use language more clearly and organize their thinking. Plus things like attention, memory, and planning can all be affected by a brain injury."

So there won't be anyplace for me to go to escape.

"I don't even want to think about school," says Tyson. "I'm going to enjoy this last day of freedom."

Dad comes into the kitchen singing the theme song to *Rocky*, a boxing movie we watched over break. He punches the air and then raises his arms over his head and makes a breathy sound, like a big roaring crowd.

"Whaddya say, boys?" He holds up the video game he got me for Christmas. "Up for a little friendly Move-It Boxing?"

Tyson nearly knocks over his stool trying to beat me to the basement door. We race down the steps and each grab a controller while Dad loads the game.

"Get ready to eat the mat, Rory," says Tyson.

"You wish," I say. "I'm so mean I make medicine sick!"

"Dude. What?"

"Nothing. Just watch out. I've been practicing."

He's Baaack . . .

The first day back to school is the kind of bitter cold that makes your nose hairs crackle. From the bottom step of the bus, I jump over frozen chunks of grayish-black slush and run toward the building. The tips of my ears sting and start to throb when the blasting heat inside hits them.

The first thing I notice when I get to my locker is that Brent's is covered in decorations. Again. There's a poster in the shape of a wrestling outfit signed by his teammates. And there's a heart-shaped note that says *Welcome back!* with a little bouquet of flowers taped to it.

I guess it's happening—he's really coming back to school. This should be interesting. When I swing my locker door open, it knocks the flowers off. Great. I scoop them up and try to press the tape back onto the note. It won't hold.

"Oh, how sweet! Are those for your *fwend Bwent?*" Danny stands in the middle of the hallway with his arms crossed and legs planted wide.

I drop the flowers back onto the floor.

Just then the hallway gets really quiet. Brent walks toward us with stiff legs, his eyes focused straight ahead. Angelo from the resource room is right next to him. I guess he's Brent's one-on-one now. A couple of kids start quiet clapping.

"Hey, Brent, good to see you!" someone calls.

"'Sup, Brent," says Danny.

Brent nods at him and grips the straps of his backpack.

"Show me which one's your locker," Angelo says.

I grab my language arts folder, wishing I'd been faster about getting to class.

Ignoring the poster and cards, Brent twists his lock and says, "Right to eleven, left to fifty-eight, right to twenty-three."

I hesitate for a moment, remembering how much trouble he had with his combination on the first day of school. Then Danny whispers something to the guys with him. I turn and push through the packed hallway. Let his friends or Angelo help him if he can't get it open.

When Brent arrives late to first period, he stops in the doorway and holds up a notebook with his schedule taped to the front.

In a thick voice, he announces, "Language Arts, Room 102."

Mrs. Nash turns from the board. "Welcome back, Brent. It's so nice to see you!"

Brent doesn't move.

"Come in, come in!" She smiles and waves him through the door.

"See you at the next bell," says Angelo. He nods to Mrs. Nash and leaves.

"Yo, over here," says Danny, pointing to the empty desk between his and mine.

"Yo-yo, yo-yo," says Brent with a big grin.

He sits down and looks around the room. Almost everyone is looking at him and smiling. I pretend to be reading.

"Brent, we're doing silent reading right now," Mrs. Nash says. "Do you have a book?"

Brent unzips his backpack and pulls out every one of his folders and notebooks.

Finally he says, "Found it!" and holds up *Pickle Pete and the Relish Rodeo*.

It's a graphic novel with tons of pictures and not many words. I read it in fourth grade. Usually Mrs. Nash would make him pick something different, but today she just nods at him with a big open smile.

It's hard to concentrate because Brent keeps laughing out loud and trying to show Danny parts of his book. Kids whisper and sneak glances, and Danny looks around to see who's watching. Finally, when Brent starts humming and tapping out a beat on his desk with the edge of his book, Mrs. Nash goes over to him.

Placing a hand on his shoulder, she whispers, "Silent reading means quiet with your eyes on your own book, okay?"

Brent brushes her hand off his shoulder and says, "But I *am* being quiet. And she doesn't have a book. Why aren't you yelling at her?"

He points to Melanie with his eyebrows pressed together in a straight, angry line.

"I'm not yelling at anyone. Ms. Franklin has my permission to be working on the computer. She's preparing for the district spelling bee," Mrs. Nash says patiently.

"Well, you should tell everyone to shut up, not just me," he continues.

"I don't care for that language, Brent," says Mrs. Nash. "But, yes, silence goes for all of you."

Danny shifts his shoulders, slightly turning away from Brent. He brings his book up close to his face like he wishes he could hide in there.

I don't see Brent again until lunchtime. His loud voice draws my attention, even though our table is halfway across the cafeteria. He's arguing with the cashier lady.

"I don't know my account number, okay? Just look it up! This place is so stupid," he yells.

The lady's face is red, and Angelo leans over the register, trying to help.

"No, I do not have it written down!" yells Brent. "Do you?"

Danny, who is right behind him, moves over to the other line.

Finally Mr. Perkins comes into the lunchroom and sees the backup. He walks over and helps move Brent out of line so the other kids can get through.

"Man," says Jett, "how could he not remember his number? We've had the same ones since, like, first grade."

"Well, from what I was reading on the internet, a lot of people with brain injuries have trouble with memory," Melanie says.

Tyson gives her a questioning look.

I think about how Mr. Simms told me the same thing. Plus all the other stuff that can go wrong too.

Brent finally makes it past the cashier and heads toward his used-to-be usual table. He looks around like he's not exactly sure what to do. Finally a couple of guys make a spot for him, and he sits down and starts attacking his lunch. Angelo leans against a pillar nearby and talks to a lunch aide. Wrappers spill off Brent's tray, and he talks with his mouth full and spits food on the guys sitting near him. One of them leans away, and another actually gets up and moves.

"Hellooooo, earth to Rory," says Tyson. "What's up, dude?"

"Nothing. Just bummed to be back at school."

"Roger that," says Jett.

For the rest of lunch, I fade in and out of the conversation at our table. I can't seem to stop watching Brent. He's trying to open his milk carton, but he pulls on the wrong side of the spout, and it doesn't work. Then he yanks, and the whole top rips, which makes the milk splash out like a fountain. The kids still at his table crack up, and he quickly wipes at the spill with the side of his sleeve.

Who cares? Let it go. He's not your friend. I wonder how much he remembers about us being friends anyway. He might have completely forgotten about that day last spring. But I haven't. I know I should forgive him, especially now. But I still can't.

One by one, the other guys get up and leave Brent at the table, alone with his mess. I watch him run a finger along the scar that's almost covered by his newly grown hair.

I touch my own head in the same spot, wishing I could reach in and erase the part of my brain that knows what I'm feeling isn't right.

A Rock and a Hard Place

A fter lunch I start walking to the speech room as usual. Then I remember. Brent will be there doing whatever he's doing with Mr. Simms. I look up and down the hallway, trying to figure out where I can hide for the next hour.

Mr. Griggs comes out to close his door. "Waiting for a train, Mitchell? Aren't you supposed to be somewhere?"

I turn toward Mrs. Sullivan's study hall, where I should have been every time I didn't have speech anyway. I'm worried she'll make a big deal about me being there, but when I slip into the room and quietly take a seat, she just nods at me and marks a paper on her desk. I scan the room for Danny, hoping to keep some distance. He's sitting on the heater against the windows and doesn't seem to notice me. *Float like a butterfly, sting like a bee; you can't hit what you can't see*, Ali's voice tells me. Stay under his radar. That's all I need to do. I picture myself taking a breath and sinking underwater, hidden beneath the surface.

I try to concentrate on my homework, but I keep thinking that even though Mr. Simms isn't *my* speech guy, it feels wrong to have to share him with Brent. What if Mr. Simms ends up liking him better than me?

When two girls go up to Mrs. Sullivan's desk and ask for help on their homework, I feel a small ping hit my shoulder. I glance behind me and see Danny looking up at the ceiling. Ignore him. *Ping. Ping.* I brush my ear, and a small white glob of paper falls onto my lap. Spitball. Nice. I look up toward the front of the room, but Mrs. Sullivan is focused on the girls' work.

I turn around in my chair and say, "Knock it off, Danny."

"Sowwy, baby, don't know what you're talking about. Whaddid I do?" He shrugs with his palms up.

"Take a guess," I say.

"Mr. Mitchell, this is a quiet study hall," says Mrs. Sullivan.

Everyone turns to look at me. My face gets hot, and I grip my pencil until it almost breaks. I picture steam blasting out of my ears like a cartoon character.

There's a sharp knock at the door, and everyone looks to see who it is. A woman from the office gives Mrs. Sullivan a note.

"Rory Mitchell, come here, please," she says.

What now?

"Mr. Simms would like to see you in his office. Isn't that where you usually go for study hall, anyway?" she asks.

"Yeah." It *was*.

"Well, your presence is requested," she says, handing me the slip of paper.

As I'm leaving the room with my things, Danny calls, "Bye, Wohwy! Don't forget the bathroom pass!"

I hear Mrs. Sullivan telling him to stop, but the other kids are already laughing.

I walk through the deserted halls as slowly as possible. When I get near the speech room, I hear Brent's monotone voice and stop to listen at the edge of the door.

"This is so stupid! Why do I even have to be here?" Brent says.

"I know you're not happy about this," says Mr. Simms. "But checking in with me is part of your transition plan, remember? You're here so we can work together to structure your time and organize your schoolwork."

I don't want to be caught eavesdropping, so I move into the doorway and clear my throat.

"Hey, Rory, there you are," says Mr. Simms. "I was surprised when I didn't see you here after lunch."

Brent is scowling, his hands gripping the tabletop.

"Rory, Brent, you guys know each other, right?"

We exchange nods.

"I, uh, thought it was his day," I mumble in explanation, pointing at Brent.

"Well, yes. Technically true," says Mr. Simms. "But I think it's important that we get Brent caught up on the biography project. We need a very clear plan moving forward." He looks directly at me, eyebrows up and head nodding, forcing me to agree.

"Okay." I sit down in the chair farthest from Brent, which isn't very far since the room is so small.

"So, Brent." Mr. Simms claps his hands. "What do you know about Muhammad Ali?"

Brent lays his cheek right down on the table and closes his eyes.

Mr. Simms gently taps the table with his finger.

Brent opens one eye and says, "Boxer."

Great. This should be interesting.

Partners

I open my research folder and spread out the pages of notes. Brent squints at my handwriting and groans. "I have a headache," he says, pressing on the sides of his forehead.

You're welcome. He gets to jump into a project that I've already started. I should be the one with the headache.

Mr. Simms turns out the overhead lights and flicks on his desk lamp.

"Is that better?" he asks.

Brent grunts a response.

"Rory, why don't you tell Brent what you've done so far?" He leans over and whispers to me, "Give me some good *r*'s, okay?"

I try to give Mr. Simms a snarky look, but he responds with an annoyingly calm smile.

I sigh and look over what I've written. "Well, I guess my notes are kinda set up by what happened during diffew— different years of Ali's life," I say.

"I've got a great idea," says Mr. Simms. "Let me help you guys make a chart."

He gets out a big piece of paper and tapes it to the wall. Then he divides it into two columns. Over the first column he writes YEARS. The second one he labels EVENTS.

"Brent, come on up here and start filling in some info," he says, handing him a marker. "Rory, what year was Ali born?"

"Nineteen fowty-two."

"Okay, good. Brent, write that down."

Brent takes the marker from Mr. Simms and holds it in his fist.

"One. Nine. Four. Two," he says, slowly writing each number. He stands back and stares at the date. This is going to take forever.

"I'll do the events, okay?" I stand up and write *born* in the next column with my own marker.

"What else, Rory? What can you tell Brent about Ali's childhood?" asks Mr. Simms.

I give Brent the basics, like that his name was Cassius Marcellus Clay Jr., and someone stole his bike and that's how he got into boxing.

"Is that true, about his bike?" asks Brent.

"Yeah. And his family didn't have a lot of extra money," says Mr. Simms. "Think about that for a second. Can you imagine how angry it made him to lose that bike?"

Neither of us answers. I pick at a loose thread on my jeans.

Finally Mr. Simms says, "You know, people deal with anger in a lot of different ways. The important thing, I think, is to not let the anger take over. Ali channeled his anger into boxing. Sometimes when I'm angry, I put on my headphones and blast Metallica. The music takes over, and after a while, I don't feel so mad. Right, Rory?"

"*Right,*" I say. I wish I could chill out to some tunes right now.

"I can't listen to loud music anymore," says Brent. "It gives me a headache. Everything gives me a headache."

"Oh, of course," says Mr. Simms. "Heavy metal's probably not the best idea for you at the moment. But wait. I know something you might like. You guys sit down. I promise this won't hurt. All you have to do is close your eyes and listen." He goes over to his computer and cues up a song.

"This one's by Guns N' Roses," he says. "They're awesome."

"'Patience,'" I say, naming the song after the first few bars.

"You got it! Now relax and let this flow over you." He turns the volume down low.

It is a pretty great song. Calm and smooth. Nothing too intense. We sit there, letting Axl Rose tell us that with a little patience, things will slow down and work themselves out. Brent massages his forehead. Mr. Simms closes his eyes and tilts his face to the ceiling, mouthing the words. When the song ends, we sit in silence.

"Can I go now?" Brent asks.

"You know, speaking of headaches," Mr. Simms says, ignoring his question, "did you know that a lot of boxers suffer from them? All those hits to the head."

I look quickly over at Brent. I'm not sure if Mr. Simms should be talking about heads getting hit.

"Like me," says Brent. "Head versus car."

I bite my lip, thinking about the crying episode at the Salmon Brook place and hoping there won't be a repeat.

"Wanna see one of Ali's all-time best knockout punches?" asks Mr. Simms.

"I guess," says Brent.

I scoot my chair around to get a better view while Mr. Simms pulls up a video on YouTube. He mutes the volume and presses play.

"Here it is in slow motion. 1965. Muhammad Ali versus Sonny Liston. Ali had taken the heavyweight title from Liston the year before, so this was the second time they fought. And watch this—BAM—and Sonny's down! Some people called this the Phantom Punch, and they said maybe Liston took a dive. But just look at it."

He pauses and starts the clip over again. "*Bam!* Nothing fake about that."

"Dude," I say. "Talk about a headache."

"If Sonny Liston were alive today, I bet he'd know just how you're feeling, Brent," says Mr. Simms.

Brent groans and slumps forward on the table, burying his head in his arms.

"Okay, time to pack up your notes." Mr. Simms points to my stuff. "Thanks for coming down to help today, Rory. In fact, I'd like you to still show up here for fourth period study hall, okay?"

Then he grabs Brent's planner. "I'm writing down a few other rock ballads for you to check out when you're feeling up to it, Brent. If you boys learn nothing else from me, at least I'll know you are getting a proper music education."

When the bell rings, Brent and I walk back to our lockers. I slow my pace so it's not like we're walking together.

A couple of kids shout things like "Brent!" and "Welcome back!" And I wonder if anyone else notices how the yelling makes him cringe.

Bus Bust

t the end of the day, I slide into the bus seat across from Jett and Tyson. Overhead vents blast hot, dry air straight onto me, and my breath fogs up the chilly window. I pull off my gloves with my teeth.

"I'm so glad our first day back is over," says Jett, shrugging out of the camouflage parka his uncle got him for Christmas from the army surplus store. "I miss break already!"

"Vacation's kind, but this grind hurts my mind," sings Tyson, tapping the back of the seat in front of him.

I smile and reach into my pocket to close my hand around the wrinkled thank-you note I wrote for Jenna. I had two good chances to give it to her today, but I chickened out both times. I clear a little circle on the glass and peer out the window to see her lined up waiting to get on the bus.

Mrs. Lyle, the school nurse, is blocking the steps while she talks to the driver. Brent is behind her, looking confused. For a split second, I remember myself as a scared five-year-old and

Brent standing next to me in the bus line, saying, *Don't worry, you can sit next to me.* But when Mrs. Lyle asks for a volunteer to be Brent's bus buddy, I don't raise my hand. She ends up putting him near the front with a kid named Max who gets off at Brent's bus stop.

When Mrs. Lyle leaves, the rest of the kids pile on. I try to make eye contact with Jenna, but she's in the middle of a group of girls who're all looking down, focused on someone's new phone. There's no way I'm giving her the note now.

The bus lurches forward, and we pull away from the curb and into the gray afternoon. The girls shriek and laugh, people shout to hear one another, and the bus tires squeal and pinch as we stop and start along the road. The girl with the new phone is playing music on it, and a bunch of kids belt out: "'Cause ooooh baby, I love you!"

Then, above the noise of the song, I hear wailing, like an electric guitar is pushing in for a solo. The sound swells, and the kids who were singing fade out as they try to figure out what's going on. Brent is standing, fingers poked into his ears. The sound is coming from him.

"Take it easy, kid. Have a seat," the bus driver says. Then over the speaker he adds, "Everyone quiet down, please. Getting a little loud in here."

"Should we try to get him to do that 'take a break, count to ten' thing we saw that lady do at the therapy place?" Tyson asks me.

"You can if you want," I say.

"Shut up!" yells Brent. "Shut! Up!"

Max puts his hands on Brent's shoulders. "Dude, sit down. You're gonna get kicked off the bus."

Brent swats him away but does sit. Then he leans forward and grabs the sides of his head, rocking back and forth.

"Stop it, stop it, stop it," he chants.

"Hang on, buddy. You're almost home," says the driver.

Brent starts to cry. The bus gets quiet, with everyone either staring at Brent or pretending not to. The only sounds are grinding gears, squeaking wheels, the whooshing heater, and a whimpering Brent.

"What's his deal?" asks someone behind me.

"Guy needs to chill," says someone else.

They don't understand about his brain injury. I could try to explain a little bit, so they'd know about him feeling overwhelmed and stuff like that. But then I remember Brent saying *total loser*.

My chest tightens, like it did that awful day last spring. When Brent had the chance to make things better for me, he did the opposite. I keep my mouth shut.

When we arrive at my stop, I rush to get off. As the bus pulls away, kids scatter into the cold, biting wind.

"See ya!" calls Tyson, sprinting down the sidewalk.

"Bye, Rory," says Jenna, turning toward her street.

"Wait, Jenna!" I grip the note.

"Yeah?" She turns back around.

"Um, I, um." *Spit it out, Mitchell.* "Thanks for the gift."

"Oh, sure. It was just a little . . . It was nothing."

"I'm so*rry* I didn't get you anything." I've been practicing that.

"No, of course not. I mean, why would you? I just happened to see the *R*, and I thought of you. Because of your name. Rory. Which, duh, you get that. So really, it was no big deal," she says all in a rush.

"Oh. Well, anyway, it was nice of you." I shove the folded, slightly damp paper at her, and she glances at it with a smile and tucks it into her mitten.

We both stamp our feet against the snow-packed sidewalk.

"Wow, it's so cold!" she finally says at the exact moment I say, "Guess I'll see you."

But neither of us moves.

"So, that was awkward, what Brent did on the bus," she says.

"I know, right?"

"I feel bad for him. It must be hard coming back to school after such a long time."

"Hmm," I say.

I wonder how she'd feel if he'd treated her the way he'd treated me—or if she'd been humiliated by him like I was.

A gust of wind swirls Jenna's hair around her face. "Okay, I'm really freezing now. I'll see you tomorrow, Rory."

"Bye." I jog home, replaying her words: *I thought of you.*

"Come in here, Rory. I need to ask you something," Mom calls as I hurry through the front door, slamming it against the cold.

"Yeah, he's home now. I'll find out and call you back," I hear her say into the phone.

"What's up?" I ask, grabbing a bag of pretzels from the pantry on my way to the kitchen.

Mom is stirring honey into her tea, which smells like spicy oranges. I sit on a stool next to her.

"What just happened on the bus?" she asks.

"How do you know about that so fast?"

"Mrs. Milliken was waiting for Brent at his stop, and the driver told her that he'd had some trouble with the ride home. Did you notice anything?" she asks.

"Yeah. It was kinda loud on the bus, and he all of a sudden stood up and went like, AAAAAAAHHHHHHH!" I do my best to imitate the wailing sound.

Mom covers her ears. "Okay, okay, I get the point! Then what?"

"He was holding his head and telling kids to shut up."

"Did you do anything to help him?" Mom asks.

I can tell that she wants so bad for me to say yes. And she can probably tell that the answer will be no.

"What was I supposed to do, Mom? He was completely flipping out."

"You could have talked to him or tried to distract him . . . anything! Did you just sit there and watch?"

"Well, someone else was assigned to help him." I shrug and pop a pretzel in my mouth. I did exactly what he would have done for me. Nothing.

Mom shakes her head. "I told you that today might be hard for Brent. I'm disappointed you didn't step up to help a friend, Rory."

I jump to my feet, and the stool tips over with a loud *thunk* as I slap my palms on the countertop. "Mom! How many times do I have to tell you? He's *not* my fwend. He means nothing to me."

Mom blinks slowly, once, twice, three times. Then in her scary-calm voice, she says, "I'm going to let you pick up that stool and go take a break in your room."

She walks out of the kitchen.

"Unbelievable," I say to myself. "*He* acts out, and *I'm* the bad guy."

I stomp on every step going up the stairs and slam my door shut. I load up Avenged Sevenfold's "Hail to the King" and put my headphones on so I can turn it up and tune out the world.

Each time the run of notes at the beginning riff repeats and crescendos, I picture my head growing, popping, expanding. It's going to burst. My big, fat, alien forehead bobs along to the throbbing rhythm of the music.

I pick up my guitar and squeeze the neck, plucking hard on the strings as I try to disappear inside the crowded chords. But it's too hard. Too complicated. The vibrations zing up my arms and press into the base of my skull. It feels like my head will never come back down to normal size. Like nothing will ever be easy again.

Breaking Point

I stay in my room until Dad comes home with dinner and I'm called downstairs. Mom and I sit across from each other, but we're both turned to the side so we're not facing head on. Mom usually drags Dad and me into a steady stream of chitchat at the table, but tonight she's silent.

Dad looks back and forth between us and clears his throat. "The General Tso's chicken is a little spicy tonight, huh?"

Mom nods. Our silverware clanks and thuds. We sip our drinks. Mom asks for a napkin. Dad passes her one.

Then Dad turns to me. "How was the first day back after break, Rory?"

"Uneventful." I keep my eyes down.

"I wouldn't exactly say that," Mom says.

I stand and pick up my plate. "He asked how *my* day was. It was uneventful, and now it's done. I'm done."

I clunk my plate down in the sink and head back to my room. Neither of them says anything or follows me. I'm on a balance beam between relief and dread, because my parents can really settle into the silent treatment when they want to. I listen to a whole playlist of songs and then decide I might as well get ready for bed. But when I come back from brushing my teeth, Mom is sitting on my comforter. Here we go.

She nods for me to sit down, her hands hidden in the deep pockets of her sweater. "So Dad and I talked."

I join her and brace for the lecture about being disrespectful. Mom stands up, goes to the window, and doesn't say anything else.

"And?" I ask.

"I've never been an eleven-year-old boy, Rory," she finally says.

"Um, I didn't think you had?" I'm confused.

"And I've never been the mom of one either. I'm—it's hard for me to always understand what you need." She flips open the locket around her neck and taps the baby picture of me inside. "I haven't been keeping up, have I?"

I get up and stand next to her at the window. We watch one of our neighbors and his dog romping and playing in the snow on their front lawn across the street. So simple. So easy.

"You do okay, Mom," I say.

"But there's a lot I don't know, right?" She goes over to the desk and gathers pens and markers into my pencil holder. "And that's okay, Rory. It's okay to not tell me everything. But if there's ever something you *want* to talk about . . ."

She comes over and gives my upper arms a squeeze. "That's it. That's all I'm saying. Sleep well."

As she walks to the door, I think about how crowded it feels in my head, all these swirling thoughts competing for space. Maybe unloading some of them will keep me from exploding. Because even though listening to music helps in the moment, it doesn't erase the thoughts forever. And I can't exactly live my life with some heavy soundtrack on continuous repeat.

"Mom, wait."

I turn back toward the window and talk to her reflection in the glass. I think I'm going to tell her only about Danny and the milk shower, but once that's out, I keep talking. I tell her about hiding out in Mr. Simms's classroom on study-hall days and all the names I've been called because I couldn't say my stupid *r* sound. I tell her about Brent being friends with Danny and his group, and them calling me a loser so many times. I tell her almost all of it.

When I'm done, I turn around. Mom is clenching her fists.

"I'd love to get my hands on that Danny kid," she says. "That kind of stuff is not okay, Rory. I don't get how people can be so awful. What I *really* don't understand is why Brent would suddenly act that way toward you! You guys have been friends for *years*! It doesn't make any sense."

I stare down at the rug. Saying that stuff out loud was like cutting the tie lines to a hot-air balloon. The pressure is lifting and starting to float away. But there is one big thing still tethering everything down.

I sit on the bed and twist the edge of the sheet around my fingers. "I used to go to the bike path, like, all the time with Bwent."

Mom scoots next to me. "I remember. Then he got into that wrestling club, and it seemed like you stopped going."

"But it wasn't because he was busy. We had a big fight."

I wrap my arms around my knees and watch the snow falling outside. Today isn't at all like that day last spring. It was warm enough then to leave my hat and gloves at home, although my hands were freezing by the time I got to the bike path. Brent was already there with a couple of guys from the team. Right away one of them started up, telling me that this wasn't a place for babies who couldn't talk yet. Brent said nothing. Didn't even say hi to me. Laughed with the rest of them.

Mom is waiting patiently beside me, so I start talking.

"Some kids teased me about how I talk. And Bwent was laughing with them. At me. I got so mad. So I told them all that he still sleeps with his teddy," I confess.

I remember clearly how Brent immediately stopped laughing, his eyes wide with hurt and surprise. In that instant I saw the old Brent again, the one who trusted me. The one I used to trust. I wanted to suck the words back in, but it was too late. Then slowly his eyes narrowed—smaller and smaller—until they practically disappeared into two thin angry slits.

"And then . . . he told them . . ."

I look away from Mom. Her hand is over her mouth, and she's shaking her head.

"Brent got up in my face and said, 'And you wet the bed.'"

Mom gasps, and I still can't look at her.

It happened at a sleepover. I'd woken up totally humiliated with no idea why or how. Too much soda before we went to bed? Sleeping too deeply? All I knew was that it was one of the most embarrassing things that had ever happened to me. Brent had promised he'd never tell a soul.

But that day he told Danny and those other kids all the details, including how it had happened the month before at his house. I heard the words *Pampers* and *Huggies* as I biked away.

"So that's it. I'll always be called *baby* now. Nothing will change that," I say.

"Rory, that's not true," she says, turning my shoulders so she can look right into my eyes.

The relief of having it all out in the open finally sets the hot-air balloon free. I feel lighter.

Mom continues, "Things like this don't last forever. You're not a baby. But you do have some growing up to do. You weren't innocent that day on the bike path. You need to own up to the role you played in all this."

"But he sided with them and laughed at me!" *Mayday! Balloon deflating.*

"You shouldn't have told them about the teddy bear." Her eyes soften. "Mr. Bear-Bear."

"I know that," I say, and tears start. "I know, I know, I know! But I was so mad that he was hanging out with all these new guys and not me. He was one of my best fwends."

Saying it makes me realize what a fake I've been every time I've said I don't care about Brent. I press my hands against a sudden belly cramp. "I can't believe I said I never wanted to see him again, and then he almost . . ."

Mom hugs me tight until I calm down, and my breath slows to normal. Then she pulls back to look at my face.

"Listen to me," she says. "The accident had nothing to do with you. That's why it's called an accident. You can't control things like that. But what you *can* control are your actions toward Brent now. What have I always told you?"

"Take a jacket?" I say with a little smile.

"No!" She laughs and bops my head. "Treat other people . . ."

"How I want to be treated," I finish.

"Yes! Never forget that. And nice *r*'s, by the way."

"Thanks. Sometimes they just pop out like that." It still always feels like a surprise, like a present that maybe I don't deserve.

"Hey, Guns N' Roses?" Mom asks, pointing to the album cover showing on my computer.

"Yeah. You know them?" I ask.

"Know them? They're classic!"

She wiggles the mouse and scrolls through the tracks.

"This one is my favorite," she says, clicking on it.

She blows me a little kiss and closes the door behind her as "Sweet Child o' Mine" starts to play.

Man-to-Man

On Valentine's Day, I get up early to sit at my desk and write out the card I got for Jenna. Not that I'm expecting her to give me anything. If she does, though, I don't want to be caught empty-handed like I was at Christmas.

But I can't decide what to say. It's like the thank-you note all over again. I try thinking about how Jenna's a good friend and how I feel when I'm around her. I have no idea how to match my thoughts up with words. So far, I have *To Jenna*. I start tapping out a rhythm with my pencil. I *tap tap* on my metal *R*, then *tap tap* on the blank side of the card. *Tap tap. Tap tap . . . tap . . . tap . . . tappity tap tap*. Nothing comes to me. This isn't working.

Suddenly there is a different tapping.

"Hey, Rory, you're up early," says Dad, knocking on my door.

He's dressed for the gym because he always works out before he goes to the hospital. I flip the card over and slide it under a stack of old papers.

"Yup."

"Whatcha working on?" he asks.

"Oh, nothing." I try to cover the squeak in my voice with a cough.

"Things are good at school?"

"Mostly." Maybe one-word answers will move this along.

I wait for him to leave, but instead he comes in and sits on my bed.

"Really? Because Mom told me some things." He rolls a pair of my socks into a ball and tosses it to me.

"Oh." I bobble the catch. Talking to Mom about all that stuff had felt good. But it's different with Dad.

"I, uh . . ." He clears his throat.

We pass the sock ball back and forth a few times.

"I was wondering how things are going with Brent. If you guys are, well, what it's like now that he's back at school," Dad asks.

I think about all that's happened in the last month. The story about Brent screaming and crying on the bus spread around the school as fast as you could hit send. And even though his mom has driven him every day since then, it's like Brent has a magnet on him that attracts trouble wherever he goes. In the lunchroom I heard Danny say, "Guys, let's get out of here before Freak Show comes in." And when Brent stood up in class and said, "I have to pee!" everyone laughed. But he wasn't trying to be funny. He looked confused.

"It's so messed up, Dad. He made fun of me, and now he's the one being made fun of. It's all flip-flopped," I say.

"You know, Rory, it's never fun to be the odd man out." Dad tosses me the sock ball again.

"Tell me about it."

"Look," he says. "You don't have to be friends with everyone. Just, you know, try to remember that all you guys are basically on the same team. Everyone has different skills that they bring to the game. You need to figure out when it's the right time to go for the shot and when to stick with an assist. Listen, I get it. I know it's hard to always do the right thing."

"You kinda sound like Mr. Simms," I say.

"Yeah? I knew I liked that guy." He covers the top of my head with his big hand and gives it a squeeze.

I smile at him.

"All right, you going to show me what you were working on or what?" He winks and taps the corner of the valentine.

I pull the card out and turn it over so he can see.

"I don't know what else to say." I focus on my pencil, avoiding his eyes.

"Ah, Jenna. She's a nice girl. You two are . . . ?" Dad hesitates.

"I don't know. I don't know if she likes me back."

"Hmm. It's tricky, isn't it? You know, you're much more mature than I was at your age. You're somethin' else."

I sneak a peek at him. It feels so good to hear him say that, like that moment when muscle memory kicks in, and I can play a song without thinking.

"Thanks, Dad."

"Well, don't thank me. We both know all your maturity comes from Mom."

We grin at each other. He walks over and looks out my window.

"Huh. Looks like it's warm enough for Mr. Garland to be out on his porch again. I should have checked on him after that last big snow. I'll bet Valentine's is a lonely day for him, his wife gone and all."

I hadn't thought about that. I try to picture Dad without Mom, and it feels like looking in a broken mirror. I just can't see it clearly.

"Anyway," says Dad. "Don't worry too much about what to put in that card. I have a feeling Jenna will like whatever you have to say."

I hope he's right.

I follow him downstairs and spend some time before school pounding out "Yankee Doodle" on the piano for Mr. Garland, hoping the sound gets through our buttoned-up storm windows.

"Where are they?" asks Tyson, stretching his neck to see the entrance of the cafeteria. His back is against the lunch table, and he's bouncing three plastic-wrapped flowers on his knee.

"Relax, Romeo," says Jett, pointing to the swinging doors that lead to the kitchen. "Check your six."

Tyson and I turn to see Melanie, Asha, and Jenna coming toward us. What were they doing in the kitchen?

"Happy Valentine's Day," Asha says.

They all giggle as Jenna plops a small canvas shopping bag onto our table. Melanie is holding an ice-cream scoop in one hand and a bunch of spoons in the other, and Asha has a stack of clear plastic cups.

"What's this?" I ask, peeking into the bag.

"A surprise for Valentine's Day! Root-beer floats!" says Asha.

"We came in early and the lunch crew let us keep the stuff in the fridge," Jenna adds, pulling out a tub of vanilla ice cream and a two-liter bottle of root beer.

"Sweeet!" says Jett, pushing his lunch tray to the side. "Gimme!"

"Dude, manners," says Tyson as he stands up and motions for the girls to sit. Then he clears his throat and recites a new rhyme as he hands each of them a flower.

"Roses are red, violets are blue; of course you love me; why wouldn't you? I'm slick; I'm smooth; I'm mighty fine; I've got more game than Saint Valentine." Tyson takes a bow.

Jett makes a gagging noise, but the girls are all smiling.

"Awww, that's so nice," says Asha. "Yellow for friendship!" She and Jenna tap their yellow roses together.

"Thanks, Tyson," says Melanie, cupping a hand around her red one.

"Our lunch table is the best!" says Jenna, waving her flower.

It would be the perfect time for me to give Jenna my card, but I didn't think to get one for each of the girls like Tyson did, so instead I pat the side pocket of my cargo pants where it's hidden and join Jett in chanting "Feed me!"

Asha passes out the cups, and Melanie scoops big mounds of ice cream into each one. Jenna walks behind us and reaches over to pour the root beer. The cool, sweet liquid fizzes as the blobs of ice cream pop up to the top. When she gets to me, she pours too fast and the frothy liquid climbs up over the top of my cup.

"Whoops! Quick, Rory! Sip!" she says. I suck in the foam, and it tickles and burns on the way down.

I try to say "yum" but it comes out as a burp. At first I'm embarrassed, but Jenna sits down next to me and laughs until she snorts. Then she fills her own cup and says, "Cheers!"

We all tap our drinks together, and I watch the root-beer bubbles let go of the sides and float to the surface.

Heavy

After lunch Brent and I arrive at the speech room at the same time. We've gotten used to taking turns with Mr. Simms.

Some days, I work on my homework or music while Mr. Simms talks to Brent about organization and planning or helps him with classroom assignments. They spend a lot of time practicing ways for Brent to remember stuff better. And sometimes Mr. Simms will set Brent up with an "attention task" and then get me to work on my *r*'s while checking to see if Brent can ignore what we're doing.

Today Metallica's *And Justice for All* album is playing when we get there and "Eye of the Beholder" is on. Mr. Simms is tapping two pencils on the table, and I grab a ruler and join in on air guitar.

"Jam with us!" Mr. Simms says to Brent, handing him the pencils.

Then he picks up his travel mug and starts singing into it about freedom of choice and doing things your own way. He's really going for it. His neck veins bulge out and everything.

After the song ends, Mr. Simms turns the music off with a sigh. "Okay, time to do some work, guys. Mrs. Nash asked me to check in about how you're getting along with research for the biography project. And Mrs. Lucas wants me to help you with strategies for remembering metric conversions, Brent."

Brent hums and taps his leg. "I'd rather do Metallica than metrics."

Mr. Simms beams. "Good one!"

Brent looks confused.

"That was a funny play on words. Remember how we talked about higher-level language skills?" Mr. Simms asks.

"I don't know—was there a memory trick for that?" says Brent.

"Ha," I say, realizing he made another joke.

"I can't believe you guys are teasing me," says Mr. Simms. "You'll thank me someday for all that I've taught you. Now, show me what's up with the project."

I pull out our folder and a thick book I got from the town library. "We've made it to 1967."

Mr. Simms opens to the page we'd bookmarked. It shows a sketch of Muhammad Ali entering a courthouse next to a white army officer.

"Okay, right," says Mr. Simms. "So you're up to where he was convicted of draft evasion for refusing to fight in Vietnam. Rory filled you in on that stuff?"

"Yeah, but that part is boring," says Brent. "Can't we just show a bunch of his fights and be done with it?"

Mr. Simms presses his folded hands against his lips. There is a long pause before he speaks again.

"Let's try something new," he says. "You two stand up with your arms straight out in front of you."

We look at each other and Brent raises his eyebrows, but we do what he asks.

"Way out," Mr. Simms adds, pulling until our arms are fully extended. "Think you can stay like that for the next five minutes?"

"Sure," says Brent.

"Absolutely," I agree.

"Could you do it even if you were holding something?" he asks.

"Yeah," I say. "Five minutes? No biggie."

Mr. Simms nods and starts a timer on his watch with a *beep*.

"The government came down hard on Ali," he says, hefting a big book off of his reference shelf and laying it on my upturned hands. "His lawyers had to work for years to prove that Ali's belief—that fighting a war was against his religion—was a valid reason to refuse the draft."

The muscles along my forearms instantly tense up under the weight of the book.

Mr. Simms gets a second book and balances it on Brent's hands. "Plus the boxing commission was really angry about him not joining the army. Remember what I told you about that, Rory?"

"They took away his heavyweight title," I say.

"That's right. The guys in charge of the world rankings stripped it away even though Ali hadn't lost it in a fight."

While he's talking I watch the clock above the door. I've never seen a minute hand move so slowly. Is it broken?

"Okay, one down, four to go," says Mr. Simms, reading off his watch. He points to Brent's arms. "You okay there?"

"Yup." Brent gives a small shrug.

I wiggle my fingers a bit. A little twinge pulses along the sides of my hands.

"I don't get why Ali wasn't able to box," I say. "You know, while the lawsuit was going on."

Without warning, Mr. Simms plops another thick book onto the first one. My arms inch lower, and I force myself to push them back up against the weight. It's been only a minute and a half.

"Well, Ali's managers tried to set up matches for him. But you need a license to box, and state after state refused to issue him one because he had an arrest on his record now."

After he gives Brent a second book too, Mr. Simms says, "The guy had been making millions of dollars in the boxing ring. But while his court case was going on, the only work he could find was giving talks at universities and colleges, for a fraction of the money. His boxing career was at a complete standstill."

I roll my neck and take a deep breath, trying to ignore how jiggly my arms feel. Mr. Simms picks up the book I brought, and I brace for the extra weight. But he starts reading from it instead.

"Let's see, that ban lasted until . . . 1970, when his lawyers proved that the New York boxing commission had licensed a ton of other people who had been previously convicted of crimes. Once a judge decided the commission's treatment of Ali had been unfair, New York and all the other states who had denied him were forced to reinstate his license."

Another thirty seconds has gone by. We're halfway there. What's inside these books, gold bars?

"So it was over? He could box again? And no jail time?" I ask, trying to distract myself from how the bottom book is pressing into the soft skin on my forearm.

"Well, at that point his federal case was still being appealed. So he wasn't exactly *free* free. But no, he wasn't in jail either. And yes, he finally had the legal go-ahead to compete."

"This is starting to feel kinda heavy—not gonna lie," says Brent, lowering his arms slightly.

"Congrats, you guys! You made it three minutes!" announces Mr. Simms. Then he slips two more books from his shelf.

"Not another one!" I say. My shoulders burn. I roll my hands gently side to side, but it doesn't help.

"My fingers feel a little numb," says Brent. "Is that normal?"

"Here's the thing," says Mr. Simms, ignoring us. "The commission didn't reinstate the heavyweight title they'd taken from Ali. By that time Joe Frazier was the champ, and Ali had to beat him if he wanted to win the honor back."

Plop. A third boulder lands on my arms. I grit my teeth.

"Of course one of the first things Ali did was try," says Mr. Simms. "But he was more like a clumsy caterpillar than a floating butterfly at that point. He was totally out of shape and out of practice, and his body-brain connection had gotten sloppy."

"Sounds familiar," says Brent, grimacing as Mr. Simms lays a third book on his stack too.

"March 8, 1971. Ali's first fight against Joe Frazier. There was a huge audience—they called it the Fight of the Century. And guess what?" He holds up two more books.

"Oh, no, no, no," says Brent. "The other guy won?"

Boom. My arms are trembling, and Brent squeezes his eyes shut as we each get a fourth book.

"Yup," says Mr. Simms. "Because Ali hadn't taken the time to do the serious training he needed. So he ended up losing the match. But he knew that with a lot of hard work and perseverance, he could try again."

Mr. Simms pauses, and I steal a glance at the clock.

"It's been four minutes. Still think you can hold your arms out the whole time?" he asks.

"Not looking good," I say through clenched teeth.

Brent shakes his head.

"Ali called for a rematch right away," says Mr. Simms, lifting the top two books off each of our piles.

It feels incredible—so much lighter.

"And he started doing the work, the *real* work, to win his title back." Mr. Simms takes away another book from each of us. Only one book and thirty seconds left now.

"It's amazing how quickly something can feel heavy, huh?" he asks. We nod.

"I wanted you guys to feel something that would remind you of the weight attached to this part of Muhammad Ali's life," he continues. "He was carrying a *lot*. And every obstacle added to the burden. It wasn't fair for him to have to hold more than anyone else because of his religion or his race. Understand? Not all his fights were big, splashy money-making performances."

"Time!" shouts Brent, dropping his arms and the last book.

I gratefully do the same.

"You can't always predict how things are going to go," says Mr. Simms, pointing for us to pick up the books from the floor. "But you have to keep trying. Fall down seven times, get up eight."

"Did Ali say that?" I ask, rubbing the feeling back into my arms.

Mr. Simms smirks. "That one cannot be attributed to him. But he sure did live it."

The period's almost over, so I start packing up our notes.

"Ooh, let me pull up a great song to play you guys out of here," says Mr. Simms, clicking around on his computer screen.

When he finds what he's looking for, he hits play and sings along to the song, repeating over and over about getting knocked down but getting up again.

Brent and I laugh at him because he's bouncing around and being such a goof. When the bell rings we head to the door, and I step back to let Brent go first. He turns and looks directly at me for the first time since he came back to school.

"Thanks, Rory."

Backfire

At the end of the day, the hallway buzzes as kids shout weekend plans at each other and rush to leave. At my locker, I undo the pocket flap button on the side of my cargo pants so I can easily pull out Jenna's card and give it to her on the bus. I really want her to have it. Even though all I've added is *From Rory*. Real poetic stuff.

My heart starts pinballing when I see her and Asha coming down the hall toward me, their heads tipped together. Asha looks up toward the ceiling and lets out a burst of laughter.

"What's up?" I ask.

"Asha's making fun of my nightmare!" Jenna says with a smile. "The pig we're fostering for the farm sanctuary got through the fence last night, and I had to chase him for, like, an hour!"

"The *what*?" I ask.

"Exactly!" says Asha.

"Could I come see it when we get off the bus?" I ask. I mean, what's a better cover than wanting to see someone's foster pig?

"Well, uh," says Jenna.

"My mom is picking us up today, Rory," says Asha. "Melanie and Jenna and I are gonna hang out at my house before Max's party."

"Captain Max?" I say.

Max is the kid who "helped" Brent on the bus. He lives near him in one of the big houses with the small yards. His indoor soccer team voted him captain, and he brings up his "leadership role" at least once every bus ride.

Jenna looks down and fiddles with a button on her backpack. "Yeah," she says.

"He's a pretty good guy," says Asha.

"Who else is going?" I ask. Not that I want to be invited.

"Well, I think pretty much his soccer buddies, plus, you know, a couple of girls to even things out," says Asha.

"Makes sense," I say. I set my backpack on the ground and start shuffling my folders around, pretending like organizing my homework is much more interesting than the first boy-girl party I've heard of.

"I'm sure we won't be there long," says Jenna.

"Why not?" asks Asha. "I heard his mom hired a DJ and everything."

"Okay. Well, have fun," I say, fighting to keep my voice light. *Never let 'em see you drop.*

Brent walks up to his locker just then. The girls are saying hi to him when Danny comes around the corner, yelling "Fri-day! Fri-day! Par-tay at Max's!"

"Max is having a party?" asks Brent.

Oh, no. I kneel down to fake-tie my shoe. *Just stay quiet, Brent! Stay invisible.*

"Who wants to know?" asks Danny.

"Is it an after-school thing?" asks Brent. "I'm supposed to go right home, but I could ask my mom."

"It's not an after-school thing, exactly," says Danny, snorting. "It's a cool-kid thing. So you're not invited."

"Dude! Rude much?" says Asha.

Danny mimics her, and I stand up. Brent looks like he wants to crawl inside his locker. Jenna looks upset too.

"Yeah, shut up, Danny," I say before I can think it through. "Leave Bwent alone."

A sickening smile spreads across Danny's face. His laugh starts low and grows into a cackle, like a deranged bird.

"Oh. My. God," he says, gasping for air between bursts of laughter. "That is the funniest thing I've ever heard! B*w*ent, you got yourself a baby bodyguard?"

"No!" Brent says, slamming his locker shut. He turns to me and spit-whispers, "What're you doing?"

"I'm, um, t*r*ying to help. This guy's being a je*r*k." I'm not giving Danny any more *r* ammunition.

"I don't need your help," Brent says, his face right up next to mine. "I don't need anyone's help!"

He storms off, weaving side to side and banging into kids on his way to the door.

I stand there like a sunken rock, watching the river of kids flow around me.

"Dude!" says Tyson, pulling me into the bus seat with him and Jett. "What's this I hear about you stepping to Danny Pulaski?"

"It was nothing. He was being a jerk as usual. So I told him so." I sound braver than I feel.

"Oh, please tell me you're joking," says Jett, rubbing his forehead. "Talk about a rookie mistake, private!"

"Look, the guy basically told Bwent that he wasn't cool enough to go to this thing at Max's tonight. All I did was tell him to shut up."

"Whoa, whoa," says Tyson. "Back up. You were defending *Brent*?"

"What's up with that?" asks Jett. "I thought you said he ignored you for the WWE kids since, like, way before he got hurt, right? You need to forget about that guy, the same way he forgot about you."

"I know, I know. Won't happen again, believe me," I say.

"Seriously, Rory," says Tyson. "Be careful with Danny. He's not gonna forget this. Dude has serious issues."

I can't believe I started trouble with Danny by speaking up for Brent. Maybe I'm the one with the issues.

A Lonely Job

Back at home I lie on my bed, spinning the valentine for Jenna by its opposite corners. I couldn't catch a break today. The harder I tried to do something right, the more I failed.

"You okay in here?" Mom asks, coming in with a small pile of clean laundry.

I groan and flip over onto my stomach, shoving the card under my pillow.

"Tough day?" she asks. She sits on my bed, making me roll to the side.

"Hey, how's your biography project going?" She taps one of the books on my nightstand.

I sit up a little. "Mom, did you know that Muhammad Ali gave up his boxing title and almost went to jail because he didn't want to fight in Vietnam? People were so mad at him."

"Yeah, I guess I kind of remember hearing about that," she says. "He said it was against his religion, right? A lot of young men felt the same way. It's called being a conscientious objector. Not a popular stance at the time. Must have been very difficult."

"Do you think he thought about changing his mind sometimes? Just going along instead of making waves?" I ask.

"Oh, Rory, I'm sure he had doubts. It would have been impossible not to. I guess his personal convictions were stronger than the pressure to do what other people wanted. You know what Grandma used to say?" she asks.

"What?"

"Being good is a lonely job." She smiles at me.

"Huh. I believe that one."

"I'll call you when the pizza gets here," she says. "Put these clothes away, okay?"

Friday night chores and a movie with my parents. "Stings like a bee," I say to Ali, who stares back from the cover of a book.

A little while later, I hear the doorbell ring, and Mom calls me down to dinner. The movie is kind of hard to follow. It was Dad's choice—lots of guys in hats waving guns around and jumping into cars. I'm half paying attention and deep into my third slice when the doorbell rings again.

"Who's that?" asks Dad. "Did you order backup pizza?"

"Ha—you wish. I'll get it," says Mom without pausing the movie. "I have no idea what's going on anyway."

I hear a familiar voice. It's not the pizza guy.

A moment later Mom walks back into the living room with her arm around Jenna's shoulders.

"Rory, you have a visitor," she says with a ridiculous grin on her face.

I scramble up off the couch and pull Jenna into the kitchen.

"Hi," I say, flipping on the light. "What happened to Max's?"

"Yeah, well. It was kind of boring, honestly. So I left." She shrugs.

"By yourself?" I ask.

"Yeah. I hope it's okay I walked over here. Your house is so close. Oh, I'd better text my mom," she says, reaching into her bag.

Mom walks into the kitchen carrying our dinner plates as Jenna puts away her phone.

"My mom's gonna pick me up in half an hour. Is that okay, Mrs. Mitchell? She'll drive right by here on her way home," Jenna explains.

"Sure, Jenna," says Mom. "Want some pizza?"

"No, thanks, I already ate." Jenna pats her stomach.

"Okay, well, let Rory know if you're thirsty or need anything and he'll get it for you. Right?"

"Yes, Mom. Thank you. I've got it," I say. *Leave us alone*, I tell her with my eyes.

Mom putters around the kitchen a little more while Jenna and I stand there looking anywhere but at each other.

"So . . ." Jenna gives one of the stools a spin, then giggles and grabs it when it tips.

"Um, want to see my room?" The *r* comes out pretty smoothly, and I relax a little.

"Sure," says Jenna.

"Leave the door open!" calls Mom.

"Mom!" I holler. I'm glad Jenna can't see my face as we walk up the dim stairwell.

"I'm sorry I'm interrupting your movie. I should go," says Jenna, hesitating at my doorway.

"No! I mean, it's okay, I wasn't that into it anyway."

"Okay, good," she says.

I flick on the light and move the pile of clothes off my recliner so she can sit down. I balance on the edge of the bed and try to smooth out the rumpled comforter.

"So, what was Max's like?" I ask.

"I guess it was okay. Melanie and Asha were having a good time, but I thought most of the guys there were kind of basic." She leans back.

"Yeah? I bet Melanie was missing Bwent, though, huh?" I ask.

"Not really. The more she learns about him, the more she's like, *meh*. Not because of his brain injury or anything. Mostly because of stuff like what happened today. We all hated the way he talked to you." Jenna peels off her coat, releasing a whoosh of her golden candy smell.

"That's actually one of the reasons I wanted to come over," she says. "To tell you that I think it was great that you stuck up for Brent. Even though he wasn't cool about it."

"I guess," I say. "Tyson and Jett think it was stupid. They think Danny's gonna take it out on me."

"Well, I know that whole crowd has basically been jerks to you all year. Including Brent, before he got hurt anyway. That's why I thought it was even cooler that you did that."

"Huh. Thanks." I decide not to elaborate on the fact that *she's* actually one of the reasons I spoke up at all—I was trying to impress her. At least that part worked.

For a while neither of us says anything. Then I go over and start "Paradise City" on my computer, clicking the volume up a few ticks.

Jenna kicks off her boots and puts her feet up on my bed, tapping them in time to the music.

"I like this a lot," she says. "Way better than the techno the DJ was playing at the party."

We listen for a while, and then, too soon, the doorbell rings.

"Rory, Mrs. Kim is here!" calls Mom.

Jenna takes her time slipping her boots and coat back on.

"So, anyway, sorry I invited myself over here, Rory."

"Don't be! I like hanging out with you." *Did I just say that?*

"I guess I'll see you Monday." She turns toward the door.

"Wait!" I go to my bed and get the card. "Happy Valentine's Day."

"Oh! Thanks," she says, taking it from me. "Um, sorry I don't have anything for you."

"Well, I already owed you one." I point to the metal *R*.

"Jenna, time to go!" her mom calls. Then she adds something in Korean.

Jenna rolls her eyes and then smiles at me. "She just said 'that door better be open.'"

We share a nervous laugh and I walk her out to the top of the stairwell.

"See ya," she says, bouncing down the steps.

"Okay, bye!" I call after her.

I go to my window and watch as they drive away, their tail-lights looking back at me in the dark. When they get to the corner, the blinker clicks on and off, winking.

And in This Corner . . .

O n my way to class, I try to be as invisible as possible, but someone shoves against my left shoulder, sending me spinning.

The guys were right—Danny did not forget about me calling him out. The payback started right after Valentine's. He'd slapped a folder out of my hands, and when I bent over to pick it up, someone else nudged me and I fell over. It's gone on for weeks.

I turn to try to figure out who pushed me this time, but all I see is the back of kids' heads as they walk away. It doesn't matter where I am or even if Danny is there. His army is everywhere. Right before I get to Mrs. Nash's classroom, a foot slides out in front of me and I trip and hit the wall. It's gonna be a long spring.

"Okay, students!" Mrs. Nash calls to us after the bell rings.

She has to speak up to be heard over the rain that's drumrolling on the dark windows. "To your seats, please!"

When we're quiet, she holds up her pointer finger. "First, before we begin, I want to take a moment to wish Melanie Franklin the best of luck in the upcoming district spelling bee."

Melanie blushes as Mrs. Nash plucks one of the bright-green shamrocks off the front bulletin board and hands it to her. "We're very proud of the hard work you've done to get this far."

"Thank you," Melanie says quietly.

We all clap, then Mrs. Nash holds up two fingers. "My second announcement is *also* about working hard. You have exactly one month from today to complete your biography projects. So be sure to take advantage of today's partner-work day. Remember that the presentation counts as *thirty percent* of your final grade. And please be creative. I want lots of visuals! I want music! Whatever you do, do not bore me—or worse, your fellow students—by just standing up there and reading what you've written."

The room is silent, all of us foggy from the rain and how early in the day it is.

"Look alive, people!" she says, clapping her hands. "Partner up and get to work. I'll come around to see how far along you've gotten."

A chorus of squeaks from wet shoes and shuffled chairs follows. Most kids push their desks together. Brent and I leave a space between us. I can't stop thinking about how stupid I was, that day I defended him, to believe that there might be some tiny piece of our old friendship left. And how quick he was to make it painfully clear that there wasn't.

For a while we both look at our own notes, ignoring each other. It's weird without Mr. Simms there to help. But we have to get this project done somehow. Besides, once it's finished, I'll never have to speak to Brent again.

"I guess we could show some of those video clips—a couple of the fights and stuff?" I say, breaking the silence.

Danny looks over at us and fake-coughs the word *baby* just loud enough for me to hear. Brent shrinks away from me, head down, and starts doodling in his notebook.

"Whatever," he says.

Danny squints at us and gives Brent the tiniest nod, like he's rewarding him for pulling away from me. Then he looks right at me and shakes his head. We're both targets, but I'll always be the one in the middle of the bull's-eye.

Later on in the speech room, Mr. Simms helps us plan out everything we need to do between now and the day our project is due. Brent writes the details into the special organizer that he's been using since he came back to school.

"You've been working hard, Brent," Mr. Simms says, looking at a page full of check marks and color-coded lists. "You're really keeping up with this planner. How are the headaches?"

"Um, better," he says. "Not so bad anymore."

"Good. I think you're ready for these, then." He hands over two CDs with scratched covers. "Metallica and AC/DC. Let your education continue. Proceed with caution, though. Don't want you overdoing it."

"Cool." Brent slides them into his backpack.

"Speaking of feeling better, I noticed the wrestling team is doing some off-season conditioning in the gym after school. Have you been able to join them?" asks Mr. Simms.

Brent's smile flattens. "Doctor still says I can't."

"Ah. I'm sure the guys miss having you around," says Mr. Simms.

I snort. "Doesn't seem like it."

"What's your problem?" Brent snarls at me.

"Hey, whoa, what?" asks Mr. Simms.

"I'm getting better, you know," Brent says to me. "I'm not going to be a loser forever like you."

"Brent! Not appropriate," says Mr. Simms.

For the millionth time, I wish I could take back standing up for him that day. He's a bigger jerk than ever.

"Just so you know, kids make fun of you constantly. You know Danny calls you Fweak Show, right?"

"Rory! Enough!" Mr. Simms crosses his arms and stares at us, slowly shaking his head.

My mouth goes dry.

Finally Mr. Simms says, "I'm really disappointed in both of you."

I study a hangnail that's been bugging me all day and with a quick yank, tear it off. A dot of blood pools quickly, and I stick my finger in my mouth, pressing my tongue against the cut.

Mr. Simms sits back and rubs his eyes with his thumb and pointer finger. He looks up at the clock. "You know what? I think we need a break. Speech time is over."

"What?" I say. There are twenty minutes left in fourth period.

"What are we supposed to do?" Brent asks.

"Go to the library and work on your project. Neither of you deserves any more of my time or energy right now."

He ushers us out the door. When it shuts and latches, the click echoes inside me.

"Didn't want to be there anyway," mumbles Brent.

I stay quiet and follow him to the library. I see a couple of kids from study hall, probably working on their projects too. I want to go off on my own, but Mrs. Dailey, the librarian, asks if we're biography partners. She sends us to two open computers tucked in the back corner on the far side of the reference section. Brent puts his head down on the table, and I look up pictures of Ali. When I get a good one, I copy it into our file.

On the other side of the tall shelves, I hear laughing.

"No, no, seriously, dude. Check it out. Can you imagine the two of them doing a project together?" asks a voice.

Max?

"I'm Wohwy, and dis is my fwend Bwent," Max says, speaking low and slow.

I sit perfectly still, wishing I could block the sound. But Brent straightens up, wanting to hear.

"Yeah, and I'm Brent, and I'm going to pick my nose in front of all of you because I'm a total moron now," says another mocking voice.

Danny. Max laughs.

Brent's hands clench. He's breathing funny. I grip the table edge and close my eyes, wanting to disappear.

"Maybe they should do their project on Brent's missing brain cells!" says Danny.

Brent pushes back and knocks his chair over. In three steps he's around the bookcase. By the time I get there, he's grabbing Danny's shirt, crumpling fistfuls of fabric.

"You think that's funny? You think I'm stupid?" Brent shouts.

He lets go of Danny's shirt and punches him. Danny tries to grab Brent's arms, but then he starts swinging too.

Max shuffles around, making space for them to keep going.

"Fight!" Max yells out into the library.

Brent's fist smacks Danny right in the jaw. Danny lets out a sound that's part pain, part surprise. It's like watching one of those

Ali videos, but this time the footage isn't grainy, and I can hear every sound amplified in stereo.

Even though Brent threw the first punch, he's staggering now like one of Ali's worn-out opponents. But Danny's the opposite, and he morphs into Ali, floating on butterfly feet like the blow gave him extra energy.

Danny pulls an arm back high, his fist loaded with bee-stinging power. My mind goes into hyperdrive, and my body springs forward.

"Stop! Stop it!" I say. "Not his head! Don't hit his head!"

All I can think about is stopping that punch. I jump on Danny and grab him in a weird hug. Caught off guard, Danny stumbles and hits the floor with a thud. I'm sprawled on top of him.

"Okay, you boys knock it off!" yells Mrs. Dailey.

I never knew her voice could get that big.

"That is *enough*," she says, pulling me up by my arm. "This is the library, not a mosh pit!"

I'm a little surprised she knows what a mosh pit is.

Brent paces around the small area, flicking his hands and muttering. Danny stays on the floor, rubbing his shoulder.

"I'm—," I start to apologize, but Mrs. Dailey flashes me an angry look that keeps me from saying more.

"Save it for Mr. Perkins," she says. "All of you. Let's go. *Now!*"

Crime and Punishment

I've never been sent to the principal's office before. At least not unless I was delivering something for a teacher. It's not like I imagined. At first we stand against the wall, like a police lineup. Through his office window, we see Mr. Perkins talking to Mrs. Dailey.

After a while Mrs. Dailey comes out and whispers something to one of the secretaries. Then Mr. Perkins calls Max in alone and the rest of us are told to sit on a bench at the back of the main office. My guess is Max is going to get a lighter sentence since he wasn't physically fighting. I squeeze my eyes shut. What was I thinking?

The secretary makes a big deal of calling our parents.

"Yes, I'm sorry for the inconvenience, but I'm afraid we do need you down here right away," she says into the phone. Between calls she looks over at us and shakes her head.

My mouth is so dry. I wish I could get a drink of water from the cooler, but I'm too afraid to ask. When Max walks out, his head is down and he's holding a bright-green detention slip. He flashes it at Danny with a shrug.

Over an intercom Mr. Perkins asks the secretary to let him know when all our parents have arrived. The regular office activity goes on around us, and I can't decide if I should wish for the time to speed up or slow down.

Brent's mom gets there first. She rushes over and hugs him.

"Are you hurt, are you hurt, are you hurt?" she asks in one big burst.

"No, Mom. I'm fine. I'm okay," he says, pushing her off.

The secretary pulls up a chair for Mrs. Milliken next to the bench.

My parents walk in next. I'm surprised and horrified that my dad is here too. Mom barely nods, her mouth set in a straight line, jaw muscles bulging. Dad refuses to look at me. Mom puts a hand on Mrs. Milliken's shoulder, and Brent's mom reaches up and covers it with her own.

We wait a while longer, but no one shows up for Danny. Finally Mr. Perkins comes out and greets our parents. Dad shakes his hand and apologizes before he even hears the story. Mr. Perkins tells Danny to hold tight and ushers the rest of us into his office.

Brent, his mom, and I take the seats, and my parents stand behind us. "Okay," says Mr. Perkins. "Obviously this is very serious. You boys know we have a strict policy against fighting on school grounds."

Brent stares at his shoes. I nod. I feel sick, like that time I ate expired yogurt.

"Brent, I know how hard you've been working on your back-to-school transition plan. So what happened today?" Mr. Perkins says.

"Danny and Max were being jerks," he says. "I'm not stupid, you know. It made me so mad to hear them saying stuff about me. I had to do something."

He bangs his fist on the arm of the chair. Mrs. Milliken pats his knee.

"Rory, what's your role in all this?" asks Mr. Perkins, shifting his attention to me. "It's such a surprise to see you here."

"Those guys made fun of both of us," I say. "Saying how bad our pwoject would be, stuff like that. Then, uh." I hesitate, not wanting to tell them that Brent threw the first punch. "Then the fight happened."

Brent looks over at me and nods a little.

"But why did you get involved?" Mom asks. "We've told you a million times to walk away from this kind of thing. Walk away and get an adult. What were you thinking?"

I twist around to look up at her. All eyes in the room are on me. How can I explain? How can I tell them that in a split second, I saw Brent as Ali, and Danny as a heavyweight boxer going for a knockout punch? And how in that same instant, I connected Brent's brain injury and Ali's Parkinson's disease, and realized how bad it could be for Brent to take another hit. I'm not sure that would make sense to anyone but me. So I stick to the simple version.

"I couldn't let Bwent get punched in the head," I say at last. "I just couldn't."

Doing Time

I can't believe it. My first offense, and I get suspended. Two days. Brent got the same thing. I'm not sure what happened with Danny, because we left before either of his parents got there.

Mr. Perkins actually seemed to feel bad when he handed down our sentence. "Sorry, our policy is very clear," he said, shaking Dad's hand again.

At least they're counting the rest of today as day one. Dad did not say goodbye to me when he got in his car to head back to work.

My ride home with Mom is also totally silent. I wish she would say something. Anything.

When we pull up to the house, I head to my room. I have no idea what to do. Nothing like this has ever happened to me. I'm so relieved to be home and have the whole thing over that I suddenly start to cry. I bury my face in my pillow, and it all comes pouring out.

The phone rings a few times, and Mom's low voice murmurs below me. Dad comes home early, and I crack open my door to hear what they're saying. I can make out only a few things, including the word *punishment*. After a while I hear their footsteps on the stairs. I slip the door closed and rub my eyes with my sleeve. The door creaks open, and they come in and sit on either side of me on the bed.

"Rory," Mom says, leaning over to kiss my head, "Dad and I have a few things we want to say to you."

I grab the edge of my comforter.

"First of all," Mom continues, "this better be the last time we get that kind of a call from school, ever."

"It will be!" I almost start crying again.

Mom looks at Dad and nods.

"Right, my turn," he says, rubbing his hands up and down his thighs. "So, um, guess we'd better cut back on the Move-It Boxing, huh?"

There is a *tiny* hint of a smile in his eyes. I lean over and press my face against his shirt. He wraps his arms around me.

"I'm so, so so*rry*." I push out the *r*'s with all my breath. "I just . . . I didn't know what else to do." I don't say that I would do the same thing again if I had to.

"Rory," he says, pulling away to look at me. "Fighting is wrong. I know you know that. But—"

"But—," I interrupt. I need to make them understand.

"*But*," Mom says, "you did the right thing today."

Dad nods.

"Wait, what?" I can't believe it.

"Okay, well, we'd all be happier if things had gone differently, but you had to make a split-second decision. In the end you stood up for someone who needed help, and it's really hard to be mad at you for that," Mom says.

"Yup," says Dad. He squeezes my shoulder. "You can hold your head up on this one."

"No more fistfights, though. Promise?" Mom says.

I cross my heart with my finger. They both hug me and then go back downstairs. I'm alone again.

I'm floating and falling all at the same time. I lie on my bed for a long time. Getting up, even to grab my guitar, feels like too much effort. I think about Ali, waiting all those years for his court case to be finished. He doesn't look tired in any of the videos I've seen of him, but he must have been, sometimes. Hanging out in the gray area between right and wrong is exhausting.

The next morning Mom wakes me early.

"Rory! Get up!" she calls from downstairs. "This is not a vacation day!"

I groan and struggle to my feet. I wonder what she has planned.

Breakfast is biscuits and sausage. I start to think I might get off easy, but Mom squashes that thought as soon as I'm done eating.

"Go get dressed," Mom says. "You've got a lot of work to do."

All morning long she has me scrape gunk off the bottom of the oven. When I mention that the oven has a self-cleaning button, the look she gives me makes me shut up and work faster. At about ten o'clock, the doorbell rings.

"Right on time," says Mom. "Come with me."

I slip my hands out of the rubber gloves I'm wearing and follow her to the door, curious. It's Brent and his mom. I take a step back.

Brent holds our biography project packet in one hand and his *Who Was Muhammad Ali?* book in the other. Mom waves them inside. She and Mrs. Milliken hug.

"I've just put on a fresh pot of coffee," Mom says, and they walk into the kitchen.

Brent and I stand in the foyer. He kicks his toe against the closed door.

"I can't believe you tackled Danny," he says. One side of his mouth lifts up.

"I am in *so* much twouble," I say.

"Me too."

"*Sorry*," I say.

I'm not talking about us getting in trouble for fighting. Brent's eyes pull open a little, and I wonder if his surprise is more about my *r* sound or my apology.

"Me too. I'm sorry too," he says, looking right at me.

I breathe it in like I've been drowning and just found a pocket of air.

After a few moments, he lifts up his book and says, "Um, I guess we're supposed to work on our project now."

Then he reaches into his jacket and holds up his phone. "I made a bunch of playlists. Metallica. AC/DC. Guns N' Roses."

A grin comes from deep inside me. "I have some ideas of songs we could use too."

"Cool." Brent smiles back.

"Let's just hope Mrs. Nash likes AC/DC, and that she focuses on the *A*, and not the *C* or *D*," I joke.

"What do you mean?" Brent tilts his head to the side.

I pause, waiting the way I've seen Mr. Simms do when he lets Brent think something through.

"Oh! Ha. I get it," he finally says. "That we'll get an A."

"C'mon." I turn and start walking toward the stairs. "Let's do this."

Free

When I get to the bus stop the next day, Jenna and Tyson rush over to talk to me.

"Hey, how was juvie?" says Tyson, punching me on the arm.

"Rory! Are you okay?" asks Jenna. "We missed you!"

The whole bus ride to school, kids ask me questions, and for once I don't mind the attention.

"Hey, Rory! I tried to call you, but apparently you were in solitary confinement," says Jett when he gets on at his stop. "Did you really tackle Danny?"

I tell the story over and over, skipping the details about what Danny and Max actually said and how afraid I had been. People tell me the fight is all anyone can talk about.

"What happened with Danny?" I ask. "He was still waiting when I left."

"Dude, Danny's dad came into the school right as we were lining up for the bus. You could hear the yelling all the way down in the gym," says Tyson.

"I actually felt bad for him, having to go home with his dad so mad like that," says Jenna. "Anyway, we heard he got two days, same as you. And Max only got a detention. Which is totally not fair, since he and Danny started the whole thing."

"Yeah, but my champ finished it," says Tyson, patting me on the back.

When I walk into language arts, Brent looks me in the eye and nods. We had a really good time working on our project at my house. I hope things keep going the same way at school.

After first period the buzz calms down, and everything goes pretty much back to routine. When I see Danny in the hallway, he walks right past me like I don't exist, which is perfect. In math class Asha passes me a note that says *I'm glad you're back!* But there's still one person I haven't seen yet.

After lunch I take the longest route possible to get to the speech room, thinking about the last thing Mr. Simms said to us. *Disappointed.* And that was before the fight! I wipe off my sweaty hands and open the door.

Mr. Simms stands when he sees me. He isn't smiling. I take one step into the room. Neither of us says anything for a moment, and I'm wondering how to start when he speaks first.

"Rory, I owe you an apology," he says.

"What? No, I'm the one who's sorry." I want him to know how much I mean it.

"Come here, come in," he says, sitting down at the table and motioning to the chair next to him. "Listen, I never should have sent the two of you out of here that day. It's a teacher's job to help students navigate conflict. I dropped the ball, and I'm sorry."

"Are you kidding me? It was totally my fault. Well, mine and Bwent's. Honestly you've helped me so, so much." Mr. Simms has been the best thing about sixth grade.

"Oh, yeah? If I'm so helpful, then why aren't you saying all your *r*'s perfectly?"

"Slow lea*r*ner," I say, letting my tongue catch up.

He grins.

"So what did you do with your days off?" he asks, shifting back in his chair and relaxing his shoulders.

"Uh, the moms made Bwent and me keep going on Muhammad Ali." I'm still dreading the presentation, but I've also begun to think that there is a small chance it won't kill me.

"We got up to his case being dismissed," I explain. I'd been happy to learn that after all that fuss, Ali had won.

"Yeah, it really helped that by the time his conviction was overturned by the Supreme Court, more and more people agreed with Ali that the Vietnam War was wrong," says Mr. Simms. "He was finally *free* free."

He pulls out the M&M's and offers me the bag. "And you're going to put in some stuff he did later in life too? After he retired from boxing?"

"That's the plan," I say.

"Okay, great. Let me know soon what you're going to say, specifically. We'll pick out the *r*'s and really get each one nailed in these next few weeks." He smiles.

I pull the beat-up index cards from my pocket and spread them out on the table. I've circled every *r* in red.

"Behold my enemies," I say. "Oh, we could also use some help with the stage lights that day. Up for that?"

"You bet, Rory. Whatever you need, I'm there."

Showtime

I can't get to sleep the night before the presentation, and I wake up tired and jittery. Mom tries to get me to eat breakfast.

"Here, at least have one of these hard-boiled eggs." She pulls a pink and purple one from the Easter leftovers.

But the thought of an egg makes me gag. All I can manage is a few sips of juice.

"Ready for the big day?" asks Dad on his way through the kitchen.

"Ready to be done."

"Hey, Rory!" Mom says. "*Ready!*"

She does that now, when she hears me say an *r*. It's happening more and more.

In homeroom, kids wander around practicing their lines and organizing props. Mrs. Nash cracks a window, letting in the smell of fresh mulch. A few notes of melody from a riff I've been working on play on a nervous loop in my brain.

After attendance we're herded into the auditorium where we'll present our projects. I stand at the back with Jett and Tyson for a while. Jett is decked out in an exact replica of General Patton's World War II uniform. He pulls out his great-grandpa's dog tags to show us. Tyson has on a tall black hat and a fake beard. Abraham Lincoln.

Mrs. Nash and another teacher fiddle with a computer onstage and check the big screen behind them to make sure the video connection is working.

"I'm soooo nervous!" says Melanie, twirling past us. "I wish I weren't so T-I-M-O-R-O-U-S!"

"Tim-or-us? I don't know what that means, but I know you'll do great," says Tyson.

"Thanks," she says, stopping. She reaches out and touches his arm. "I'm sure yours will be marvelous too."

"Just a matter of time, boys," says Tyson after Melanie skips away. "I'm reeling her in."

"If you say so." Jett laughs.

Mrs. Nash taps the microphone to get our attention. "Okay, everyone, please find your partner and take a seat. We need to start on time if we're going to enjoy all your projects today. Your rows are marked by class period, which is also the order for the day. Take a seat, take a seat."

I find Brent and sit next to him. "We good?" he asks.

All I can do is nod. My tongue is paralyzed.

"I know you've all worked very hard," says Mrs. Nash from the stage. "So without further ado, please give your kind attention to my first-period language arts scholars, starting with Livia Bergin and Aydin Uluer."

There is polite clapping as the lights dim.

Slowly we work our way through the presentations. A lot of kids are dressed up as inventors, actors, or athletes. One pair shows a pretty cool video display about Bill Gates. The funniest project is on Babe Ruth. The kid who is supposed to "hit a home run" keeps missing the whiffle ball his partner throws.

When there's just one pair left before our turn, a trickle of sweat snakes down my back.

I tap my pocket, checking that the flash drive is still there. "You have the music?" I whisper to Brent.

"Dude. Chill," he says, flashing his phone to show me.

Too soon, the last set of partners before us is onstage. They show a bunch of slides of Michael Phelps, and take turns talking about his life and his impact on swimming. At the end they play the national anthem and hold up handfuls of fake gold medals. When the song finishes, I clap along with everyone else, even though my hands are shaking.

"We have time for one more presentation before lunch," says Mrs. Nash.

Kids squirm and shift. It's gotten warm in here.

"That's us," I say to Brent.

"Students!" Mrs. Nash says. "Please give Rory Mitchell and Brent Milliken the same respectful attention you have given the others this morning. Boys, take it away."

Brent and I move down the row and into the aisle. I check my note cards one last time as I force myself up the steps on the side of the stage. Shading my eyes, I nod toward the control booth. The lights dim, and there are whispers and then shushing from the audience.

I insert the flash drive into the computer and open the file with our slideshow. The big screen at the back of the stage lights up. Brent holds his phone up to the microphone, and the growling sounds of Metallica's "Don't Tread on Me" fill the large room. A few pictures of Muhammad Ali scroll by. A spotlight shines on Brent, and he turns off the music. He narrates the next few slides, talking about Ali's early life.

A picture of Ali in one of his amateur fights comes on the screen, and the spotlight turns to me. I'm not even sure I'm going to be able to say anything, let alone what I'm supposed to. The light is hot, but I'm shivering. I grip the card and lean into the mic.

"'Clay swings with his left, Clay swings with his right. Look at young Cassius carry the fight,'" I hear myself say.

I don't even recognize my own voice. *My tongue is behaving! I might survive.*

"Preach!" I hear Tyson say in a loud, deep voice, which makes me smile and relax even more.

Brent is supposed to narrate the next slide, but he forgets. I tap my finger on his script, and once we get started again, everything goes okay. Brent explains about Ali's name change, the draft, and how he was banned from boxing. Then I switch the slide and talk about Ali losing to Joe Frazier in the Fight of the Century in 1971.

When we get up to the Rumble in the Jungle with George Foreman in 1974, I pause on a picture of Ali working out with a speed bag and motion for Brent to play the next song, "Welcome to the Jungle" by Guns N' Roses.

"All right!" someone yells. After about twenty seconds of music, Brent turns it off, and I click on the next video.

I push play. The whole screen goes blank.

The Comeback

I try hitting different buttons on the computer, but it's completely shut down. Nothing. This is a total nightmare. We're only halfway through our presentation. Mrs. Nash comes bustling onto the stage to see if she can help.

"Hey!" I hear a voice yell. "Get away from there!"

Everyone turns to follow the sound, and the overhead lights flick on. Danny is standing near the stage where the projector table is set up, holding an unplugged extension cord in his hand.

"Oops!" he says with a big grin.

But no one laughs. No one makes a sound.

Before any of the teachers can get to him, I hop off the stage and grab the cord.

"Back off, Danny," I say, plugging it back in.

The computer whirs to life, and we wait for Ali to return to the screen.

"Hey, it was an accident! *Loser,*" Danny coughs into his hand.

The only way I'm a loser is if I stay down for the count.

"It's cool," I say. "You didn't knock me out." I point to the cord and shrug.

I'm not even that mad. He smirks to cover a flash of surprise. He wants me to be upset and angry, but I'm done. I really don't care what this guy thinks of me anymore. Because I finally get that the heavy stuff he's carrying is what's making him act this way. And he must be pretty tired of it all to do something as stupid as this in front of everyone.

"You know, you don't have to hang on to all that weight," I tell him. "You can put some things down."

"What are you talking about?" He snorts and shakes his head. "Are you the one with the brain injury?"

Mr. Leigh is the first teacher to get to us. When he leads Danny toward the auditorium exit, someone starts a slow clap. Then other kids join in, and pretty soon the whole sixth grade is clapping. As the noise dies down, I climb up the side steps back onto the stage.

"Please continue, boys," says Mrs. Nash from offstage.

Mr. Simms dims the houselights, and I'm in the spotlight again.

This time when I press play, the video rolls a clip of Ali riding in an old car on a dirt road, people dancing and calling out to him as he passed.

"Fans took to the streets of Kinshasa, Zaire (an African country now called the Democratic Republic of Congo), to cheer on Muhammad Ali before his big fight with George Foreman," reads Brent.

"Ali! Ali!" the people chant in the video. All those people hoping he would win the fight.

When I hit pause at the end of the clip, Brent says, "Muhammad Ali knocked out George Foreman in the eighth round, regaining the title of heavyweight champion of the world."

I look up at the image behind me of Ali, grinning as he leans out of the car to grasp someone's hand. His smile reminds me of how people can be brave even when it's hard. I grab the microphone, and I'm steadier this time.

"'My face is so pretty, you don't see a scar, which pwooves I'm the king of the ring by far.'" Not perfect, but not bad.

Kids go wild. It takes me a second to realize they are cheering for me. *For me.* I feel like Ali must have, with all those people on his side: powerful and like he belonged.

The rest of the presentation feels lighter and more fun. Through our words, pictures, and songs, we tell the story of the champ defending his title and finally defeating Joe Frazier in the Thrilla in Manila in 1975. Then we show how he battled to both lose and win against Leon Spinks in 1978.

"Ali fought with everything he had to stay on top until he retired from boxing for good in 1981," says Brent. "And in 1984, he was diagnosed with a new opponent, Parkinson's disease."

We show a picture of Ali holding the torch at the 1996 Summer Olympics, and I talk a little about Parkinson's. Then I say how he did many more things with his life after that, including being named a Messenger of Peace by the United Nations in 1998, for all the stuff he did to help people all over the world, especially poor people.

The screen changes to an image of President George W. Bush putting a ribbon around Ali's neck.

Brent reads, "In 2005 Ali was awarded the Presidential Medal of Freedom for his 'contributions to the security of the national interest of the United States, world peace, and other endeavors.'"

Brent ends his part with a little bit of AC/DC's "T.N.T.," and he fades the music right after the song mentions winning the fight.

I step to the microphone for my final quote, one Mr. Simms helped me pick out especially for this project. We figured out through research that most people think Ali said it, but really Jesse Jackson did. But it's too perfect not to use today. Behind me is the slide of a gray-haired Ali, with his birth and death dates: January 17, 1942, and June 3, 2016.

I go slowly so I can nail the *r*. "'If my mind can conceive it, and my hea*r*t can believe it, then I can achieve it.'"

The picture fades, and Brent and I both take a bow. The kids in the audience all jump to their feet, laughing and cheering.

I glance toward the control booth. Mr. Simms is leaned up against it, grinning and clapping. When he sees me, he does a one-two punch motion. I blink and try to freeze this moment. It's absolutely perfect.

New Song

Danny got an in-school suspension for causing our presentation fiasco. And during the few weeks since then, he's pretty much avoided me. All his buddies started leaving me alone too. Jett and Tyson thought I would be way more upset about the whole thing than I was. Truthfully even the day it happened I wasn't as mad at Danny as they were. And now whole days go by and I don't even think about him. So it all kind of feels like a win.

Today feels especially good, because it's Friday and almost June. The countdown to the end of school has begun. After lunch, Brent and I walk to the speech room, kicking someone's forgotten pink eraser between us. Mr. Simms said he had something special in mind for our time together today.

When we turn the corner, I see Danny standing in front of the speech room. This better not be the something special. He straightens up when he sees us, and I pull to a stop, instinctively bracing for snark. The sound of Metallica's "Nothing Else Matters" trickles into the hallway.

"He always plays cool music," says Danny, pointing to the door. "You guys are lucky." Then he turns around and struts away.

Did that really just happen? I look at Brent with wide eyes, and he smiles and opens the door.

Mr. Simms is sitting on top of his desk, hunched over a black and white Fender Squier guitar.

"Oh, good, you're here! Listen to this, guys!" He carefully places two fingers of his left hand on the second fret and strums a chord.

"Sweet!" I say.

He smiles and holds the Fender out to me. I run my palm over the smooth wood and pluck some notes.

"After your presentation, I thought I'd give it another try," he says. "You guys really inspired me that day."

"People love to throw that word around since my accident," Brent says, shaking his head.

"I'm serious," says Mr. Simms. "When I saw you two up there doing things that were hard for you, I decided it was time to stop making excuses about learning guitar. So I got this baby and started taking lessons. It isn't easy, though." He holds up his left hand to show me his swollen red fingertips.

"Yeah. That happens till you get these." I show him my calluses, and he cringes.

"*Hard* rock is *hard* work!" Mr. Simms says, then laughs at his own joke.

I groan and play a loud broken chord.

"You just don't appreciate good comedy!" he protests.

He takes back the guitar and lays it down carefully in its velvet-lined case. Then he pushes a chair against the wall and pats the seat. "This is our stage for today. I want to practice for Step-Up, so there won't be any surprises for either of you."

I make a face.

"We wouldn't need to pwactice if someone would just announce all the kids like they used to do," I say, pointing at Mr. Simms.

"Oh, c'mon, you don't need me, Rory."

"Uh, yeah, I do. I still can't say that *r* sound in the middle of my name without totally stopping and fixing my tongue. Rohwy. Rohwy. Ro . . . ree. That's the only way I can do it, and it sounds stupid that way." I cross my arms.

"Listen. You're gonna be fine, no matter what happens. Just think, in a couple of days, you'll be living the sweet summer life of a rising seventh grader," Mr. Simms says.

"Speaking of that, I can't believe you graduated me fwom speech. I'm not ready."

"Yes, you are. I mean it. You've worked so hard, and you know what to do. It won't be long till all your *r*'s come out the way you want them to."

He points to the chair. "Hop up onstage. Let's hear you. Just relax and let it flow."

I shake my head, not believing it will ever be as easy as he's describing.

"Brent, show him how it's done," Mr. Simms says.

Brent climbs up. He raises both arms in the air and wobbles a bit. "Brent Milliken!"

"Easy, buddy." Mr. Simms reaches out to steady him. "Okay, are you going to have something with you to share?"

Brent climbs down. "Maybe. Do I have to?"

"No, but a lot of kids bring a visual with them that kind of describes what they were into this year," Mr. Simms explains. "They usually keep it pretty simple."

But it wasn't a simple year for Brent at all. He spent more time in his hospital helmet than his wrestling headgear. How could one little prop sum up all the big things that happened to him?

"Asha's not going to have anything," I say. "She says she's awesome enough. So, you don't *have* to show something. I mean, you wouldn't be the only one."

"I like that," says Mr. Simms. "Awesome enough. What about you, Rory? What's your plan?"

I point to his guitar case in the corner. "Ta-da."

"Ah, of course. Rory the rock star. C'mon, your turn onstage." Mr. Simms gestures toward the chair.

I stand up on the chair and focus, but it's just like always. I'm not Wohwy anymore, but I'm not quite Rory either. Something occurs to me that I would never have thought of when this year started. I wish Brent and I could be partners for Step-Up Day. He'd say the names, and I'd be the soundtrack. I sit down on the chair and slump onto my forearms.

Mr. Simms puts his hand on my shoulder. "Look. Perfection is overrated, if you ask me. I want you to be loud and proud when you introduce yourself. You're a cool kid, Rory. You've just got to own it."

After that, he works with Brent on making sure all his year-end assignments are organized in his planner. I grab the guitar and pick out notes one by one, softly, letting my mind blur. Soon a melody bubbles up inside me. The individual notes line up in a pattern that rises, repeats, and falls, and before I know it, they've all blended together into a new song.

One Last Fight

T he last weeks of sixth grade fly by, and suddenly we're at Step-Up. A teacher props open the side doors to the auditorium, and the full warmth and smell of June rushes in. Everyone seems a lot more relaxed than they were the day we did the biography projects. Kids are laughing and joking around, showing each other what they brought to take onstage. I'm wearing my guitar by the strap like a backpack.

A lot of kids are in their sports uniforms. Jett has his baseball glove and hat.

"What's up?" I ask him. "You on leave from the army?"

"Hey, what can I say? Spring is for baseball!" Jett replies.

Melanie joins us at the back of the room, wearing a sign around her neck that says E-N-N-O-B-L-E.

"Can I get a definition?" Jett asks.

"*Ennoble*," says Melanie. "To elevate in degree, excellence, or respect. As in, 'We are about to ennoble our status at this school.' Also, the word I got out on at districts." She makes a face and sticks out her tongue.

Tyson comes in carrying a pizza box. He opens it and shows us half a pizza.

"Dude, really?" asks Jett.

"What? We're supposed to bring in something that represents who we are. And I am truly a pizza-loving, half-full kind of guy." He spins the box and almost drops it.

As the teachers herd us to our prearranged alphabetical areas, Jenna walks by holding a small plastic cage with a stuffed dog in it. The sign hanging from it says *Adopt, Don't Shop*.

I grab her arm. "Hey, Jenna, hold up a second?"

We move into the small alcove by the side doors.

"What's up?" she asks.

"I just wanted to say . . . I hope we have some of the same classes in seventh." I grip my guitar strap to dab the sweat off my hands.

"Totally! Math was fun this year. But you're making it seem like we won't see each other before next September." She laughs. "You should come to the pool club with us this summer. You and the guys."

"That'd be awesome."

As Mr. Perkins takes the microphone and asks us to find our seats, Danny walks by.

"Ooh, are you guys boyfriend-girlfriend?" He makes a kissing noise against the inside of his elbow.

"So what if we are?" asks Jenna.

She grabs my hand and makes a face at Danny. He shakes his head and walks away, and then we're standing there, holding hands.

She looks at me, with the question simmering between us. *So what if we are?*

Before I can say anything, Mr. Leigh steps into the alcove. "Take your seats, please!"

I quickly squeeze Jenna's hand before Mr. Leigh pushes us back into the aisle. Hopefully my huge smile is saying all the words I can't.

Mr. Perkins starts counting back from ten. When I sit down, I grasp the neck of my guitar. In theory it's easy: I'm just going to hold it up, strum one chord, do what I need to do, and get out of there. And I already did a whole big presentation in front of these same kids. But the fight to say my own name is one I haven't won yet, and my nerves are revving. When I pull my hand away from the guitar, six lines are imprinted on my skin.

Some of the teachers are seated on the stage, fanning themselves and chatting. I catch Mr. Simms's eye, and he nods. I shake my head side to side. *Just go as fast as you can*, I say to myself. *Get it over with.*

I try to slow down my breathing. As Mrs. Lucas and Mrs. Nash usher the front rows up toward the stage, I chant Tyson's song in my head. *Never let 'em see you drop. Don't sink to the bottom, gotta float to the top.*

It's not long before Mrs. Lucas comes to the end of our row and has us all stand up. We walk single file past the kids who already took their turn. Tyson points at me from the G's.

I nod back at him and try to swallow. The moment is here. I lick my lips. I get my tongue ready, and I'm practically biting holes in the sides of it by the time I climb the stairs. I can at least go heavy on the first *r*.

Mr. Griggs stops us one by one at the bottom of the steps. As Sarah Merrin is shaking Mr. Perkins's hand, Mr. Griggs says,

"Okay," and waves Brent up onto the stage. The whole place explodes with applause.

Brent walks over to the microphone. I take short, shallow breaths. My chest hurts. I might actually be having a heart attack. *What if I'm actually having a heart attack?* I pull my button-down shirt away from my sweaty skin.

"Mitchell, you're on deck," says Mr. Griggs, and I stand on the top step.

"Go ahead, Brent," says Mr. Perkins, and I realize that Brent still hasn't said anything.

"I'm Brent Milliken," he says. Kids cheer and clap. Mr. Perkins waves him over for his handshake, but Brent stays at the microphone.

"I can't remember," he says, looking back at me and then out into the audience. "Did I bring something?"

"That's all right," says Mr. Perkins. "Come on over and shake my hand. Welcome to seventh grade!"

"No!" says Brent. "I was gonna . . . What's my thing?"

He sticks his hands in his pockets and pulls them out, empty.

"You're fine," says Mr. Simms, standing up. Brent paces behind the microphone, rubbing his hands through his hair. In the audience, kids are exchanging looks and whispering. Two guys in line behind me start to laugh.

I think about what I said to Danny—about setting things down when they get too heavy. He's not the only one. Everyone has stuff that's hard to carry. And maybe sometimes all you need is for someone to help lift.

"Yowah thing is with me," I say, striding to the middle of the stage. *What am I doing?*

I lift up my guitar and strum a strong G chord right into the microphone.

"What are you doing?" he asks.

"I don't know yet," I whisper. "Just follow along."

I play a quick G-C-G progression.

"While you guys studied hard," I say, "we studied hard rock."

Mr. Simms calls out, "Yeah!"

Three more chords, and I think of another one.

"Maybe you got A's, but we got AC/DC!" I holler.

I play a longer riff, then lean over to remind Brent about one of his jokes. He smiles and grabs the microphone.

"You got the metric system; we got Metallica," he says.

I'm thinking I might just burst out in a full song right there, but Mr. Perkins comes over and says, "Thank you, boys. That's great. We'll move on now."

Brent's smiling again, and he waves at all the students who are making noise for us. He walks over to the side of the stage with Mr. Perkins.

But I can't leave yet. There's still something I need to do. I sling my guitar behind my back and look down at my feet. My speech isn't perfect, and I don't know if it will ever be. But there's stuff about me that I *do* know for certain, things that matter a lot more than how I say my *r*'s.

I check in: My breath, my teeth, my tongue, my lips, my heart. They're all ready.

Loud and proud. I lift my face to the audience and say my name.

A Note About the /r/ Sound

Speech development is different for everyone, and the /r/ sound tends to be one that consistently frustrates both students and speech-language pathologists. It's considered a "later-developing sound," and clear use of /r/ corrects itself somewhere around age seven or eight in many cases.

But some people need a little extra help. If that is you, you are not alone! The exact position needed for your lips, teeth, and tongue (called speech articulators) to produce *any* sound is an act of extreme coordination, especially when talking.

There's an added challenge, because how an /r/ is made can change slightly depending on where it occurs in any given word, such as before a vowel (called prevocalic), in one of six different combinations after a vowel (called post-vocalic), or as part of a consonant blend (like the *pr* in *pretty*). When we count them all up, there are at least thirty-two separate, distinct ways that /r/ can be produced. That's a lot of darts on Mr. Simms's dartboard!

Rory's progression with mastering /r/ is somewhat typical, although it may be different from your own. He begins by saying

/r/ correctly as one sound. Then Mr. Simms helps him target /r/ in specific word positions such as the beginning (like *r*eady), middle (as in Ro*r*y), or end (such as miste*r*). As Rory masters more and more /r/ sounds, post-vocalic (after vowels) is still hard for him, especially when the /r/ follows a vowel sound that's produced in a different part of the mouth.

If you are looking for help with any kind of speech or language skills, the American Speech-Language-Hearing Association (ASHA) website (www.asha.org) is an excellent resource. Clicking "Find a Professional" on the homepage can help you connect to someone in your area.

If you read this story at the same time that you're working on your /r/, guess what? I wrote this book for you. Keep up your good work, and please remember that *how* you say something is never as important as *what* you have to say. Be loud and proud!

Acknowledgments

I'd like to shout into the microphone my heartfelt gratitude to editor Karen Boss for bringing clarity and richness to this project and for having awesome taste in music. I am incredibly grateful that Rory and I stepped into your classroom!

Thank you to the entire team at Charlesbridge, including designer Jon Simeon. Also thanks to copyeditor Hannah Mahoney. I could not have asked for better help pushing this *little story that could* over the finish line.

I am beyond grateful to my clever and enthusiastic agent, Emma Sector, who saw where I was and met me there anyway. The whole gang at Prospect Agency, Rachel Orr in particular, have been incredibly supportive. You all make one heck of a backup band.

This story exists today because of the Shoreline Arts Alliance/ Tassy Walden Awards and the New England Society of Children's Book Writers and Illustrators Ruth Landers Glass Scholarship, which both gave me the nods of encouragement I needed to keep working.

Thank you to the team at Little Pickle Press for being an important stop on this journey and especially for giving me the gift of my first editor, Tanya Egan Gibson. Tanya, thank you for asking more of me than I knew I could give and for being there when I lost my footing. You are a treasure.

This story has been around a long time, and I have many people to thank for helping me turn it into the novel you see now. Early readers who gave invaluable feedback included Deborah and Aydin Uluer, Tonia Branson, Ruth and Livia Bergin, Wendy Smith, Katie Protrulis, Eileen Washburn, and Lynda Mullaly Hunt. Justin Pistorius, Barb Lucas, and Stacy Bell fielded many questions about middle-school policies and the sixth-grade experience. Kayla Segal, a true rock star, was my source for all things guitar. Debbi Michiko Florence and Cindy Faughnan took me aside in the early days and encouraged me to hold fast to Rory's voice. The members of the Kim Keller book club and many others gave steadfast encouragement and never stopped asking, "How's the writing going?" I thank you all!

Sometimes spontaneous events can directly influence the heart of a novel. I will be forever grateful to Max Branson for showing his son a video clip of Muhammad Ali and to Jack Branson for acting it out at my kitchen table. And to Thomas Ersevim, who stepped onto the stage as a prince and sang with the voice of an angel.

To the members of Mainstream Blaze, Renegade (the other one), and the Bends: Thank you for filling my home with music and my ears with the soundtrack for this novel.

To the Glastonbury SCBWI critique group: From day one, you have been an incredible source of information, comradery, and inspiration. Thank you to dear Betsy Wittemann for starting us off and to all the talented writers who have given me insightful critiques over the years. A special thanks to Eileen Washburn for holding me accountable and always being up for anything! And to Jeanne Zulick Ferruolo for the confidence boost and the encouragement to "just keep writing."

To the Red Barn Writers: Jill Dailey, Michele Manning, Kristina O'Leary, Paula Wilson, Jessica Loupos, and Holly Howley. My Pleiades sisters, you've guided me with love and friendship in clear skies and dark clouds. Surrounding myself with your incredible talents has made me a better writer and person. Holly, thanks to you especially for being an early teacher and for asking me the most important question of my writing career: "*Why not?*" TBS would like you all to know that the world awaits your stories.

Cheer Squad roll call: Thank you to Teams Tandon, Merrifield, and Holden for shaking pom-poms of encouragement. My namesake aunt, Nancy Garland, has always been there to spot me in this and all of life's endeavors. Teammates Jennifer Bowen and Angie Bell have never failed to be my steady bases. Jason Tandon has helped me stay in formation and commiserated with me on how hard it can be to get to the top of the pyramid. Varsity co-captains Tonia Branson and Deborah "Friend" Uluer both deserve trophies. Tonia, thank you for being there every step of the way as we navigated our own character arcs through early motherhood and beyond. Debi, you light up my soul. When you were my only friend in all the world, it was enough.

John and Carol Merrifield are parents so blatantly amazing you'd never see them in a middle-grade novel. "Once-a-once-a-time" you gave me a blank book and asked me to "tell you a story." Thank you for being my first audience and for encouraging me always, in every way.

Finally, deep love and gratitude to the people I'd choose to have on my quaranteam any day. Kate and Vijay, thank you for not letting me give up. You make me want to tell stories with happy endings, which is what I wish for you, forever.

And most of all, thank you to my dear curmudgeon Rajnish. You have lovingly supported me in every way one human being can support another, asking only, "Show me the book." Honey, here it is.